The Guest Who Refused to Leave

The Guest Who Refused to Leave

The Story of the Sunset Hotel/Crystal Bay Hotel

MaryAnn Illingworth

ISBN: 1532836708
ISBN 13: 9781532836701
Library of Congress Control Number: 2016906943
CreateSpace Independent Publishing Platform
North Charleston, South Carolina

To the most wonderful grandchildren in the world:
Grace, Benjamin, Ava, Elle, Maia, Balin, Evan, Luke, and Rowan.
May you always love to read and be curious about the world around you!

Table of Contents

Map of the Pinellas Peninsula from the early 1900's

Pinellas County 2016

Sunset Hotel at the beginning of the 2013 renovations

Photo courtesy of Mark Tong

Good friends are hard to find, harder to leave, and impossible to forget.

AUTHOR UNKNOWN

Clara

I saw the sea fog rolling in quickly as I started my walk. I had chosen to live on Boca Ciega Bay for the beautiful views, so for me the fog enhanced the beauty of the area. The cloudy wisps created a magical effect that muted sounds and quieted the world. The swirling mist almost seemed to be a portal that could open to times other than the present.

The heavy fog made it difficult for me to see even across the street, and it created a feeling of eeriness as familiar landmarks faded in and out of view. I had considered staying home, but I knew once I reached the old Sunset Hotel Clara would be waiting for me. She has a sixth sense about things and the fog would not be a problem for her. Walking with her is always a delight. She has been in this area for years and knows wonderful stories about its history and the people who have lived here.

I've only known her for a short time but we have become good friends, and it seems as if we have known each other forever. I do have to admit, though, that in the beginning our relationship had gotten off to a rocky start.

I saw Clara for the first time a few months ago as she stood on the porch of the old hotel. She seemed to be talking to someone inside the building. Taken aback to see anyone there, the woman piqued my interest. Rumors were floating around that the building was going to be renovated, and we all hoped that might be true. It is a stately old structure, but as long as I could remember it had been more or less abandoned. I saw the woman look at me curiously as I walked by and I heard her laugh merrily. I assumed she must be connected with the renovation project.

A few days later I saw her again. This time she stood in the yard and waved when she caught sight of me. Surprised, I waved back. The woman intrigued me, and my imagination ran wild with scenarios to explain her.

Perhaps she had lost her home in the recent economic downturn and had moved into the empty hotel because she had no place else to go. I imagined her struggling to make a new life for herself. While it was a romantic idea, I remembered how expensive her clothes looked and her hair had been beautifully styled. She was definitely not homeless.

Maybe she had arrived from some exotic faraway place because her life had been threatened. It did seem possible that she might be foreign because her clothes looked a little different from what people around here wore. Happening upon the old hotel she realized it would be the perfect spot for her to take refuge. Then I thought about her standing in the yard, talking to people, and waving at strangers. It seemed hard to believe she was trying to hide from anyone.

As dull as it seemed, she probably really was involved with renovating the building and keeping an eye on things as they progressed. I didn't see any construction vehicles around, but they may have been requested to park off site. The workmen, in all likelihood, were inside.

The next day, as I neared the hotel, I saw the woman standing by the sidewalk. She appeared to be waiting for someone, and she had to be going to a costume event of some sort. She wore a cloche, and her dress, with its low waistline and short pleated skirt, came straight from the 1920's.

As I got nearer her face lit up. "I thought I'd missed you!" she called.

I turned to see who she might be speaking to, but no one else seemed to be around. Could she be speaking to me?

"Of course I mean you! I hoped you would walk by. I've wanted to talk with you ever since that first day when I saw you pass the hotel. Do you have time to stop for a minute?"

Stunned, I said nothing. She took my silence as agreement and asked me to join her for tea. In a daze, I followed her up to the veranda. The porch looked much fresher and neater than it appeared from the street. There were even tables and chairs that I had never noticed before. On the table closest to us sat a lovely, antique white tea set with a large pink rose on each piece. I commented on the table and the woman replied that the staff always did a lovely job.

I looked around. What did she mean by the staff? We were the only people there that I could see. I began to think that stopping to visit might not have been a good idea.

The table did look lovely. I wondered where the tea set came from; probably the woman had found it somewhere. I had no idea how she had been able to make tea because the long neglected building couldn't have running water. I felt it would not be wise to drink anything from the beautiful cups. My idea of her being homeless, in all likelihood, had been correct. I feared she would be asking me for money soon.

The woman looked at me reproachfully and stated, "I am not homeless, and I don't need money, but I do live here. I assure you the tea is perfectly safe to drink and it is delicious. You must try it. The restaurant has been on the Duncan Hines Adventures in Good Eating list for years. You don't get on that list if the food is not excellent and safe to eat."

What could she possibly be talking about? This place had been closed for years! There was no restaurant here. Even if there had been, from the way the building looked, it could not be an award winner of any sort.

"You do know the name of the hotel, don't you?" she asked. "You seem to refer to it as 'this place' a lot."

An eerie feeling came over me. How did she know what I had been think-ing? I realized that not only had she been aware that I didn't know the name of the building where we sat, but she had also known I thought she might be homeless or destitute and my concerns about drinking the tea. I had an unset-tling feeling about this woman and felt I should go on with my walk as soon as possible.

"This is the Sunset Hotel," she said proudly. "My husband always said it was the most beautiful place to stay in Davista."

Davista? She didn't have any idea where she was! We were in St. Petersburg, close to the Pasadena area. I had never heard of Davista. The woman sitting across from me obviously had serious problems. As well as not knowing her location, her clothes said she didn't know the century either. She appeared to be a nice lady and she was probably lonely. I felt empathy for her, but she wasn't my problem. I stood up, "I have enjoyed talking to you but I need to finish my walk. Thank you so much for the tea. Perhaps we will meet again sometime."

The woman looked startled and then began to laugh in the merry way I had heard the first time I saw her. "I am so sorry. Please sit down. I think I can clear all this up quickly. First, let me introduce myself. I am Clara Loughlin from Philadelphia. I did not mean to be so bold. I, unfortunately, assumed you understood more than I now realize you do. When you waved and spoke to me, I just thought you knew."

What did she think I knew? I didn't sit down, instead I moved to the steps of the porch. Looking out toward the street I saw a friend walking by. She waved and called hello. Then she took a few steps onto the lawn and asked if I needed any help. Puzzled by her question I told her I was fine.

"I'm so relieved," she replied, "I saw you standing on the porch of that abandoned building. You seemed upset and looked like you were talking to someone, but I didn't see anyone there. I thought perhaps something had happened. I'm thankful everything is okay." Then waving good-bye, she continued down the street.

I turned to Clara, "She acted like she couldn't see you. What could be wrong with her?"

Clara sighed, "I am afraid you will not like the explanation. She can't see me like you can because I'm, you might say, in another dimension. Her vision isn't good enough to see me."

I came back to my chair and sat down. I heard my voice shaking, "My friend's eyes were good enough to see me talking to you. What do you mean she can't see you because you're in another dimension? You are sitting right here on the porch; I can see you perfectly. Why couldn't she? You make it sound like you're a ghost or an extraterrestrial of some sort!"

The look on Clara's face made me very uneasy. Unthinking, I picked up my cup and took a sip of the tea. It was delicious! I took another drink, and it confirmed my first impression. This could not be ordinary tea. Then realizing what I had done, I quickly set the cup down.

Clara nodded, "I told you that you would like it." Taking a deep breath she continued, "I will do my best to try to explain. I don't know why you can see me when most others can't, but I am sure there is a reason. I don't like the word 'ghost.' To me it has an evil connotation. I'm not here to cause harm to anyone, and I am not an alien from outer space. I return to the Sunset Hotel each winter because it holds so many wonderful memories for me, and it is where I meet old friends."

What was happening? It seemed like a normal day, beautiful and sunny. People and cars were passing by on the street as they always did. However, I found myself on the porch of a dilapidated hotel, sitting across from a woman who professed to be a ghost but doesn't like the term, and claimed that others "in another dimension" are also here. One of us was having a mental lapse of some sort; I hoped it wasn't me.

Clara must have wandered away from where she lived and probably shouldn't be out on her own. I asked if she lived nearby and said I would walk her home. She shook her head no. Then I asked if she had family that I could call to come and get her.

With a note of resignation in her voice Clara replied, "I told you, I live at the Sunset during the winter. I have no family down here, but I do have a lot of friends staying at the hotel."

"Well, if that's true," I demanded, "why can't I see them? Where are they? How can you live in a building that is empty and in disrepair?"

Clara rose. "Obviously, I have overloaded you for today. I'll let you continue your walk and think about our conversation. I am sure I will see you soon, but I would like for you to do one thing before we meet again. See what you can find out about a publisher by the name of Frank Davis. He lived in St. Petersburg in the 1880's. I have a feeling it will work better if you find out about him on your own. We can talk about what you have learned when we meet again.

"I've heard getting information is so much easier now than it used to be because you can look things up on a net. I saw you have one of those little boxes that people use to carry their nets in. Everyone seems to have one of those net boxes now, even children! I'm sure you will be able to find out something interesting about Frank.

"I will see you soon," Clara said. Then she just disappeared along with the beautiful tea set and my delicious cup of tea.

Frank Davis

Photo from the St. Petersburg Museum of History

Your imagination is your preview to life's coming attractions.

ALBERT EINSTEIN

Frank Davis

I finished my walk and decided to forget about Clara and the whole experience at the old hotel. I doubted I would ever see her again. I went to bed that night and slept soundly. There were no dreams of ghosts, old hotels, or ladies serving tea. When I awoke, the events of the day before had faded from my mind. I poured a cup of coffee and took the newspaper outside to read by the pool.

As I looked through the paper a real estate listing caught my eye. The bold lettering under the picture read "Located in South Davista." Davista! Wasn't that the name Clara mentioned yesterday? I thought she had made up the name, but the word kept jumping out at me from the newspaper. I sat back stunned, and for moment I was sure I could hear Clara's merry laughter.

I was going to get to the bottom of this. Just before she disappeared Clara had told me to look up someone. I tried to recall the name. Suddenly I heard her say, "Frank Davis, a publisher from Philadelphia." I went inside and typed the name into my computer.

Frank Davis is a common name and it took me a few tries to get to the right one, but I found him. He had owned a publishing company that specialized in medical writings and studies. In 1885, he attended a conference in New Orleans where Dr. W. C. Van Bibber, the personal physician of philanthropist Johns Hopkins, spoke. The well-respected doctor had a theory that peninsulas are, by their nature, healthy places to live, and a peninsula on a peninsula would be an even better location. He stated he had found the healthiest place in the world—Point Pinellas, Florida. Dr. Van Bibber, feeling that the climate here would maximize health and longevity, proposed that a "health city" be built on the peninsula.

Frank Davis suffered from muscular rheumatism, so he decided to test the doctor's claims for himself. After spending a short time on the peninsula, he discovered that most of his symptoms had disappeared. He believed Dr. Van Bibber's theory had to be correct, and he began to write articles and books promoting Point Pinellas for its health benefits. Plus, all his medical journals carried advertisements for the area.

The publisher, being a shrewd businessman, decided to act on the doctor's proposal of building a "health city." After looking at several locations, he settled on a small town of three hundred people on the Tampa Bay. He felt sure that St. Petersburg was exactly what Dr. Van Bibber had in mind. Davis bought the electrical and trolley franchises for the town and the telephone system. Next he built a three thousand foot pier, which he illuminated at night with hundreds of lights. Finally, he formed an investment company of local men and investors from Philadelphia. He used money from the company to buy thousands of acres of land west of town, which he planned to divide and sell for development.

Things went well until the banking panic of 1907 when worried investors began to call in their loans. The money Davis had borrowed was tied up in land that was now worthless, and he had no way to repay what he had been loaned. In 1909, he had to cede control of the investment company to the major stock holder, a man by the name of H. Walter Fuller.

Suddenly a word in the article caught my attention, "Davista." It seems Fuller divided the land he had acquired into sections and named the one where the old hotel stood after Frank Davis. Clara had been correct; the Sunset Hotel had been in Davista!

I decided to go over and see if I could find Clara again. Walking up to the building I realized I had never paid much attention to it before. From the street, at a quick glance, the hotel didn't seem to look too bad, but this time I stopped and really looked at it. Everything needed a lot of work. The lawn and landscaping desperately begged for attention. The building needed new paint, and there were several areas that required repairs. Missing panes in the doors and windows made me cringe to think what might be inside. A tarp covering the ground west of the hotel probably hid a swimming pool, but I doubted anyone could swim in it. The building did its best to look regal, but it was getting very hard for it to keep up the pretense.

I didn't see Clara. Stepping onto the leaf-covered porch, I looked in the dirty windows. I saw no sign of life anywhere; the building appeared empty and deserted. Had I just imagined meeting Clara? I walked back to the side-walk and stared at the old hotel. I didn't know for sure what I had experienced yesterday. I was a little disappointed that I didn't find the woman, but I felt relieved that things were back to normal. I turned and started home.

As I reached the corner of the lot I heard someone calling for me to wait. I turned and saw Clara coming up behind me. She seemed a little winded, "There is no way I can keep up with you when you walk that fast. I am not as young as you are." Then she smiled, "I was right about things wasn't I? What did you think about Frank Davis?"

The thought flashed through my mind that Clara's presence said something about my sanity. I had come to the hotel hoping to find a ghost, or someone who pretended to be a ghost, and I had found her. That should have worried me, but for some reason it didn't. I unhesitatingly followed Clara up to the porch.

As I went up the steps I saw a table with another lovely tea set. This time there were cookies too! I sat down and looked at the tidy porch and the sparkling windows. What happened? I felt almost sure there had been nothing here a few moments ago, but now tables, chairs, and rockers sat on the porch. How had I missed seeing all these things? One of the rockers, sitting where it caught the wind, gently rocked back and forth, making a soothing creaking sound. The porch that had seemed so deserted a few minutes ago now had a homey, comfortable feeling about it.

Clara poured the tea. "I could ask about your day or your walk, but I doubt that is what you want to talk about. Did you find out anything about Frank Davis on the net?"

I nodded. I meant to answer her question, but I had just bitten into a ginger cookie that was melting in my mouth. I've eaten a lot of cookies, but this had to be one of the best. Most ginger cookies are hard and crumbly; however, this one had a soft moist texture with the perfect melding of flavors. I intended to enjoy every bite of it.

When I swallowed the last morsel I turned to Clara. I knew I needed to bring her into the twenty-first century, especially if she really did come from another dimension as she claimed. "You don't look things up on a net," I explained. "It's called the internet, and I did find him. What an interesting man! You were right about everything, and I need to apologize for doubting you."

"Thank you," Clara primly replied. She sat quietly for a few seconds and appeared to be thinking. When she spoke, instead of telling me more about Frank Davis she asked, "What is an internet? Where do you get one? How does it work?"

I shook my head, "I can't explain it. I don't really understand it myself. The internet is a way to get information and communicate with people. You don't have your own, it's something everyone shares. The little boxes you see people carrying are our phones. We communicate with them, but we can also use them to do research." I laid my phone on the table for her to see.

Clara carefully picked it up. "This is a telephone? Where is the cord? What is it connected to? How can you talk to people on it? Where do you keep information in this tiny box?"

I began to appreciate Clara's dilemma the day before when she tried to explain things to me. I decided the best way would be to show her how it worked. Taking the phone from her, I typed in the name Frank Davis, pulled up one of the articles, and handed it back to her.

Clara peered at my phone closely. Her eyes widened when she saw the words on the screen. She turned it over and looked at the back, perhaps to see if there were more words there. She held it up, as if showing it to someone, "Amazing! Can you believe it?" Suddenly she leaned forward, as if someone had bumped into her, and she almost dropped the phone. Quickly she laid it on the table. "I am so sorry! I don't want to break it." Looking around she complained, "Sometimes it just seems so crowded out here."

There were only two of us on the long porch and I knew I wasn't crowding her. I ignored the complaint and tried to steer the conversation back in the direction I wanted it to go, "Please, tell me more about Frank Davis. I read how he promoted and developed this area, purchased and lost the land where the hotel is, but what happened to him after that?"

"Poor Frank," Clara murmured, "I never met him, but my husband Thomas knew him from Philadelphia, and they occasionally ran into each other down here. Adeline, Thomas' first wife, always said she found him charming. I gather he was a wheeler and a dealer with great ideas; he just didn't stop to think his ideas all the way through.

"After losing everything in 1909, he convinced his Pennsylvania backers to invest in the purchase of thousands of acres of land north of St. Petersburg. He established a town he called Pinellas Park and divided the land into ten acre farms which he offered for sale. Things went well until fifteen inches of rain fell in August. The new land owners discovered that adequate drainage had not been installed, and they were not happy about their farms being under water. Frank had problems, again.

"Not long after that disaster he moved back to Philadelphia. He might have been right about the health benefits here, because soon after he moved back his health began to deteriorate. He died a short time later."

I took a drink of my tea and thought about what I had just heard. There was so much about this area I didn't know. I watched people passing by and wondered whether any of them knew about the events that had taken place here more than one hundred years ago. An older gentleman, wearing a suit and hat, stopped at the corner of Central Avenue and Park Street and looked around. He seemed to be trying to figure out where he was. Turning he looked at the old hotel for a few seconds. His eyes found mine and seemed to find Clara's. He smiled at us. I smiled back and for some reason I waved to him. He actually tipped his hat and then walked on.

I found the gesture to be chivalrous, something from another time. Clara looked at me with a twinkle in her eye, "I guess they were correct about Frank being charming."

Life is like a cup of tea…it's all in how you make it.

ANONYMOUS

The most popular tea in the1920s was Orange Pekoe. The term 'Pekoe' refers to the British grading system rather than the color or flavoring of the tea. 'Orange' refers to the Royal House of Orange.

MAKING THE PERFECT CUP OF TEA

- Keep tea stored in a sealed jar or tin
- Tea loves oxygen—it helps the flavor develop, so always use fresh drawn cold water in the kettle
- Warm the pot by swirling a small amount of boiled water in it
- Black teas—pour on freshly boiled water, do not over-boil it
- Green teas—use water that is just at the boiling point
- Use one teaspoon of loose tea per cup and one teaspoon for the pot
- Tea bags should steep for three and a half to four minutes and then removed
- For Loose tea the rule is the larger the tea leaf the longer the brewing, but never brew more than seven minutes. Earl Grey and Lady Grey teas need only five minutes. Smaller leaves need four minutes brewing time
- Never use a tea cozy. It extends the brewing time and can make the tea bitter Twinings Tea

H. Walter Fuller - 1915

Photo from the St. Petersburg Museum of History

If opportunity doesn't knock, build a door.

Milton Berle

H. Walter Fuller

Finishing my tea I turned to Clara, "Why did Frank Davis and his investors buy land here? Surely land closer to the center of town would have been a better choice and more desirable."

Clara nodded, "Yes, most people would agree with you, but Frank had plans to build a 'health city,' and he wanted it located by the water where the air was healthy. There were no bridges across Boca Ciega Bay to the islands, so people looked at this area as the beach. Frank believed he had found the perfect spot for healing.

"Now I have another name for you to look up, 'Walter Fuller.' You need to be aware there were two men with that name, the father, Henry Walter Fuller, and the son, Walter Pliny Fuller. These are men I knew and I think you will find them interesting. We'll see each other soon."

I realized that I had been dismissed. This time Clara didn't vanish, she just sat there drinking her tea. I said goodbye and left. Glancing back when

I reached the sidewalk, I saw Clara still sitting on the porch. She had turned toward the chair that had been rocking in the wind, and she seemed to be talking to it.

A few days passed before I found the time to research the Fullers. I knew a Walter Fuller had taken over Frank Davis' holdings, and I guessed the nearby Fuller Park might have been named for one of the men, but beyond those things the name meant nothing to me. I wondered why Clara thought I would find them so interesting. I soon found out. The Fullers had been involved in much of what went on in the early days of St. Petersburg's development. I couldn't imagine why I'd heard so little about them. I could hardly wait to talk to Clara.

When I met her again, instead of the welcoming smile I expected, she demanded to know where I had been. Her attitude caught me by surprise, and I reminded her that I had a life outside of looking up names she assigned to me. She quickly apologized, "I'm sorry. It's just I have so much to tell you and season always goes by so quickly. I hate to waste any of the time we have."

We went up on the porch but this time, instead of the usual tea service, I saw a tall narrow pitcher with small demitasse-sized cups on the table. I looked at the set curiously. "It's a chocolate set," Clara said. "It's a little cooler today and I thought hot chocolate would make a nice change."

As Clara poured, the aroma of rich, dark chocolate rose from the cups. A small bowl of whipped cream sat on the tray, and Clara put a healthy dollop in each of our cups. Taking a sip I realized this was not ordinary hot chocolate. It was a culinary experience! Obviously, there were no artificial ingredients of any kind in this drink. Something gave the chocolate a delightful flavor and I wondered what it could be. I told Clara I would love to have the recipe. She smiled. "I thought you would like it. It's the peppermint schnapps that makes it so good."

As we drank the amazing chocolate, I shared with Clara what I had learned about the Fullers and asked her to tell me more about the men. She set her cup down, "I hardly know where to start. To distinguish between them we always call the father, Walter, and the son, Walter P. I like them both very much, but I got to know Walter P. much better than I knew his father because Walter moved to North Carolina not long after I started coming to St. Petersburg.

"Walter was born in Atlanta at the end of the War Between the States. That beautiful old City had been destroyed by General Sherman during the war, and after the hostilities ended most of the residents found life very difficult. One of the biggest killers at the time was something we called consumption, but you know it as tuberculosis. In its ravaged condition, Atlanta was hit hard by the disease. No one knew what caused the illness or how to treat it, and the outcome was seldom good. Walter came down with consumption at the age of eighteen. The doctor told him that he would not live to be twenty-one and suggested moving to Florida might make his remaining days easier.

"Thankfully, the diagnosis ended up being totally wrong! Walter lived fifty-six years longer than his doctors predicted. However, Walter didn't know he had a long life ahead of him. He believed he was dying so he took the doctor's advice and moved to Florida.

"When he arrived in 1883, the eighteen year old borrowed sixty thousand dollars and used the money to buy every orange grove he could. A couple of years later a flu epidemic swept across the country, and doctors told people drinking orange juice would keep them from catching the flu. Walter made a fortune! When he turned twenty-one, not only was he alive and healthy, but he was a millionaire.

"After that successful venture Walter began looking for another opportunity to expand his wealth. He decided to buy a steamboat line. At that time the easiest way to get to Tampa from the Pinellas peninsula was by water, because there were no bridges across the Tampa Bay. Traveling by land you had to go to the top of the peninsula, cross to the mainland, and come back down the other side. The fifty mile journey took two days on a horse, but the trip could be made in two hours by steamboat. Walter felt he couldn't pass up the opportunity. He sold all his orange groves and put his entire fortune into a steamboat enterprise."

Clara reached for her hot chocolate and saw our cups were empty. She refilled both cups, again adding a generous amount of whipped cream. The hot chocolate had been a perfect choice for the day. Sheltered from the wind on the porch, we sat quietly sipping the thick, rich drink.

Finally, Clara set her cup down. "My husband said when Walter got an idea in his head he refused to see any other options. Once Walter made up his mind to purchase a steamboat line he ignored all advice to the contrary. Unfortunately, he should have listened to what people tried to tell him. Soon after he set up his steamboat enterprise a railroad line came into St. Petersburg. Trains weren't dependent on the weather or conditions in the Bay to get to Tampa. They quickly became the way to travel and move goods. Walter lost everything.

"I heard it said that Walter made eight fortunes in his lifetime and lost seven and a half of them. That may have been true, but he never let anything get him down, not even losing millions of dollars. Walter moved to Bradenton, got married, had five children, and ran a general store. He branched out into road building and did well. In 1907, he received a contract to pave roads in St. Petersburg and arrived with several hundred men and sixty mules.

"Walter hadn't been here long before he started looking for new ways to make money. After making several wise decisions, including becoming the major investor in Frank Davis' company, he became a millionaire again.

When Frank lost his shares in the investment company, Walter eagerly took over. This area was a wilderness, but land sales were going well. Walter believed if anyone could make money selling land he could, but he knew his offerings would have to stand out from the others. He hired professional planners to lay out neighborhoods and design a golf course, the first one in St. Petersburg. Walter also hoped his plans for a country club might appeal to the socially elite of the fledgling town. He advertised the area as 'The Gem of All Florida Developments.'

"In August of 1914, with the beginning of the Great War, frightened investors started holding onto their money and almost all land sales stopped. That didn't worry Walter. He told his backers the war would last less than a year, and they needed to have things ready to go when the war ended. Borrowing money from anyone he could, Walter began putting in sidewalks and paving streets in his developments. The only way to get to his property was by a narrow road called Central Avenue. Walter didn't feel the street gave the right impression to buyers. He convinced the City to widen Central Avenue to one hundred feet all the way from downtown to Sunset Park, a distance of almost seven miles, and he got the contract to do the work.

"As owner of the trolley company, he laid a track down Central Avenue to Park Street where the line turned and went north. The land Walter owned stopped at a street called Elbow Lane. He didn't want investors to find it easy to look at anyone else's property so the trolley turned around at Elbow Lane and went back to town.

"Things didn't work out the way Walter imagined. Instead of ending quickly, the war went on for four long years. Investors began to call in loans, and Walter, like Frank, could not repay the money he had borrowed. He lost everything, again. However, his Philadelphia investors, hoping to get back some of the money they had lost, loaned him enough to repurchase the land. He did so at a fraction of the original price and was back in business."

Clara paused. I realized both of our cups were empty again. This time I poured, but Clara insisted on adding the whipped cream. She took a few sips, then primly wiped away her white mustache and continued with her story.

"Around this time Walter P. joined his father in the company. Walter wanted to focus on a wilderness area at the north end of his holdings, which he liked to call the Jungle, so he let his son take over the developments around Davista.

"Walter P., who had just graduated from the University of North Carolina, started looking at how he could make their land more appealing to buyers. It didn't take him long to discover a problem. Most of the people interested in purchasing property were not from this area and needed accommodations when they arrived. If they liked the place where they stayed they tended to look at land around that location. There were no hotels near the Fullers' land holdings, so prospective investors had to stay in town and that's where they usually bought.

"It was obvious that the Fullers needed a hotel on their property. Walter P. wanted it to be something luxurious that would set an example for the type of neighborhoods they planned to develop. A beautiful hotel, full of guests and offering activities, would show people they were moving into an established area, not a wilderness. And even more important, a hotel would produce income that vacant lots didn't.

"The Sunset's location had originally been divided into five lots, but no one had shown any interest in them. Walter P. decided those lots would be the ideal site for a hotel. The location, across the street from the Park and near the water, meant guests would have the benefits of beautiful views and healthy air; and they could enjoy boating, fishing and bathing. Plus the new golf course and country club were only a short distance away. The Fullers announced they would lease the land to anyone who would promise to build a luxury hotel there."

Clara stopped and took a sip from her cup. "This is a good place to stop today, because this is when my husband met Walter. We can start here the next time."

I sat back in my chair and thought about the Fullers. I couldn't imagine losing millions of dollars over and over and not letting it defeat you. Suddenly, I noticed a tall, thin, middle-aged man standing inside the hotel! He wore a suit and looked a little like the pictures of Will Rogers that I had seen. He appeared to be paying close attention to Clara; however, I felt sure he had been looking at me seconds before.

Realizing I had seen him, the man quickly backed out of view. A little frightened, I leaned over and whispered to Clara that someone was inside the hotel. Unconcerned she replied she wouldn't be surprised. She asked what the person looked like and I described him.

Clara nodded, "Walter P. is always interested when he thinks people are talking about him."

Construction of the Sunset Hotel in 1915

Photos curtesy of the USF Archives

Your life does not get better by chance, it gets better by change.

JIM ROHN

Thomas

I could hardly wait to talk to Clara again. I found myself fascinated by the people and history around the old hotel. Tea was waiting for me when I arrived. Clara and I chatted for a bit and then she asked, "Did you know that my husband, Thomas, and his first wife, Adeline, were two of the original guests at the hotel?

"Thomas was an architect and did quite a bit of work in St. Petersburg. The town was growing quickly and by 1915 it had over five thousand people. He liked this area and enjoyed working here. Adeline loved big city life, so she chose to stay in Philadelphia with her family and friends when Thomas worked in Florida. He had planned to work here through the end of March but some things had happened that made him feel he should return home. War had begun in Europe and investors, fearful of what might occur, were stopping construction projects. For Thomas, though, something even more concerning than hostilities in Europe happened—Adeline became ill.

"While Thomas wanted to be with Adeline, returning to Philadelphia in January did not hold great appeal for him, especially with the delightful weather here. Plus, the mayor of St. Petersburg had just announced that Thomas' beloved Phillies would be training in St. Petersburg that spring. That made the thought of leaving even harder.

"Finishing up his project in January of 1916, Thomas remembered hearing several times that Sunset Park on Boca Ciega Bay was supposed to be the best place in the area to watch sunsets. He had always meant to check out the claim for himself but never seemed to find the time. One evening, shortly before his departure for Pennsylvania, he decided to get on the trolley and ride to the park.

"When he arrived, Thomas noticed something being built across the street. Most construction projects had stopped so he was curious about the structure. He could tell it was going to be something very large, but he couldn't imagine what it could be or why anyone would be building something that big so far from town.

"Thomas saw two men standing in front of the construction site and he went over to talk to them. The men were Walter Fuller and Robert Grigg. Robert had leased the land from the Fullers and proudly told Thomas about his project, a four-story apartment hotel with every amenity. There would even be a roof garden, with a dining room and refreshment parlor, where guests could enjoy the view and dine under the stars. Robert announced firmly that the hotel would be called the 'Bella Vista.'

"Walter had remained quiet while Robert explained the project, but he held a different idea about what the hotel should be named. Walter stated he wanted the hotel called the 'Sunset.' He felt that name would better place the building and its location in people's minds.

"My husband said the two men seemed to share the same ideas about the hotel and its design, but they obviously parted ways at the name. Thomas asked about the wisdom of building a hotel so far from the center of town. The men seemed surprised at his question and replied they couldn't imagine a better site. The location on the water, away from the hustle and bustle of the city, made it a healthy, quiet, relaxing place. If guests wanted to go into town they could get on the trolley and be there in a few minutes. Walter shared some of the things he had planned for the area, mentioning the new golf course just a few blocks away. That caught Thomas' interest! He had just started playing the game and loved it.

"As the men talked they found they had a common bond, Philadelphia. That was both Thomas' and Robert's home, and many of the investors in Walter's company were Philadelphians. They discovered they had several mutual acquaintances and a common love for the Phillies. Walter and Robert suggested the three of them ought to get together soon. Thomas told his new friends that he would like to see them again, but he had to leave in a few days because of his wife's illness.

When Walter heard about Adeline, he shared how both he and Frank Davis had been cured by coming to Florida. He suggested Thomas rent one of the units in the new hotel, bring Adeline down for the winter, and see if being here helped her.

"Thomas listened with interest to Walter's idea. The hotel, scheduled to open in November, would have forty apartments. There would be a few smaller units that were reserved just for prospective investors, but each of the other apartments would have at least four rooms and an electrically-equipped kitchen. There would be an elevator to make getting to the higher floors easy and a restaurant where guests could have meals.

"Thomas liked what he heard, but he wasn't sure what Adeline would think about coming to a small town in Florida. She loved city life with its activities, shopping, and luxuries. Her illness was serious and while he wanted her to be comfortable, happy, and well taken care of, he really did like it down here. Walter, being a salesman, told Thomas that units were already being rented, so if he thought he might be interested he should decide quickly. The cost of a unit for the season went from two hundred and fifty dollars to six hundred and fifty dollars, depending on the size of the apartment, its location, and whether or not meals would be included.

"To be honest," Clara laughed, "I think Thomas had made his decision the first time he heard Walter mention the golf course, but then the sun started to set. The view was spectacular! Thomas signed up for the largest unit they had, knowing they might need to bring a nurse or companion with them. He wanted to be sure they had enough room to be comfortable.

"Adeline had serious reservations about coming to Florida, but hoping the warmth might improve her health she agreed to try it. They arrived on opening day, November 29, 1916. Thomas found the worsening economy had caused some changes to the original plans for the hotel. The building had three stories not four, and only thirty apartments instead of the planned forty. The roof-top garden would be completed later, but the rest of the hotel had everything promised. Amused, Thomas saw 'Sunset Hotel' on the front of the building. Walter had prevailed.

"Robert Grigg and his wife hoped the Sunset would become the social center for the area, so they chose to manage the hotel themselves. They held their first event, a Thanksgiving Dinner, at the hotel on opening night. The Griggs invited hotel guests, friends, and people interested in the hotel to attend. The large turnout gave them confidence the hotel would be a success. After dinner, everyone got on the trolley and went to the St. Petersburg Country Club for dancing and a card party.

"Much to her surprise, Adeline found the evening to be enjoyable. She discovered that people at the hotel were as cosmopolitan as people in Philadelphia. The women wore the latest styles and knew the current trends. Adeline, with her accepting smile and gentle disposition, made a good impression on everyone. She received several invitations for upcoming social events, and to her delight she found that the mild weather meant there many more activities here than there were at home. She liked that.

"The Griggs hoped starting with a party would enable hotel residents get to know each other and help them integrate into local society. They wanted their lodgers to feel at home at the Sunset. By the end of the evening, Thomas and Adeline both felt coming to St. Petersburg had been the right decision for them."

Clara and I watched as the sun began to set. Above the trees the blue sky began to turn lovely shades of pinks, oranges, and yellows while the clouds took on hues of gray. I thought it looked lovely, but Clara told me it was nothing like it had been in the early days when you could almost see the sun set into the Gulf. It had to have been my imagination, but as the sun went down all the buildings in front of me seemed to disappear. The sun appeared to be a white ball as it sank into what looked like the water. I could have sworn I saw a flash of green just as the sun disappeared. It was beautiful!

Sunset Hotel soon after opening in 1916

Kindness is the language which the deaf can hear and the blind can see.

MARK TWAIN

Adeline

The next time I returned to the Sunset Hotel, Clara was standing by the sidewalk. Instead of inviting me up to the porch she asked if I would mind walking with her. That surprised me; Clara really didn't seem like the walking type.

As we started down the block, I knew we made quite a contrasting pair. I had on sweat pants, a well-worn but comfortable, long-sleeved tee shirt and walking shoes. Clara wore a dress with a long, narrow skirt that ended at mid-calf, a pair of black pumps, dress gloves, a hat that looked a little like a turban knotted in front, and a mink stole. I hoped no one I knew would be able to see her.

Clara looked at me disapprovingly and remarked, "I do wish you would take more pride in your appearance, it's always a little embarrassing to have my friends see you looking this way. I don't know what has happened to this younger generation!"

As we walked, Clara turned the conversation to the early days of the hotel. "You know, when Thomas and Adeline stayed in the hotel in 1916 it had little resemblance to a hotel stay today. At that time renting a hotel unit meant you were actually renting an unfurnished apartment. In fact, the Sunset was called an apartment hotel. That meant you brought trunks full of everything you needed for your stay, including clothes, bedding, linens, pictures, decorating items and sports equipment. You also had to bring your furniture. Those who planned to do any cooking needed to include dishes, crystal, cutlery, and cooking supplies. Picky eaters even brought their favorite foods.

"Trains were the only way to get here. With everything you had to bring it meant travel was very expensive and difficult. You did not come to St. Petersburg for a week or two; you arrived for the whole season. Guests were, for the most part, wealthy and older. Hotels opened before Christmas and closed the end of March. Air conditioning didn't exist at that time, and no one liked to be here when the weather got warm. You wanted to be home, unpacked, and settled before it got too hot.

"Adeline brought more than most people, partially due to her illness and a need to be comfortable, and partially to let people know she had the best. The Sunset fit her need for status. Their corner unit was one of the largest apartments and had a spectacular view of Boca Ciega Bay. Adeline could watch sunsets through their windows or from the balcony outside their rooms.

"The elevator ensured she didn't have to walk up the stairs to their third floor apartment. She could easily stay in touch with her family and friends back in Philadelphia because each unit had its own private telephone. Most people didn't have a telephone in their home at that time, let alone in a hotel. It was a luxurious place to stay.

"Adeline and Thomas, being the youngest people here, soon got to know everyone. Adeline quickly became a favorite with the older ladies. She had a good sense of fashion, and the women looked forward to seeing how she dressed each day. The other lodgers knew about her illness and were protective of her; Adeline often found herself the center of attention. She and Thomas became friends with the Griggs, and their friendship opened the doors to local society for her. She loved her time here!"

We finished a lap around the hotel and Clara suggested walking to Sunset Park. There we found a bench and sat down. Clara turned to look at the hotel and I followed her gaze. "The hotel was so lovely then. The entire first floor had a large, open, wrap-around porch where people met for tea or drinks, to visit, or to just enjoy the view. The verandas on the second and third floors could be reached from each apartment on that level. The towers at the ends of the building had lovely pergolas which you walked through to enter the roof terrace. The view from up there was spectacular and more than one sunset was toasted from that rooftop."

Looking at the hotel, I thought how sad and run down it appeared. The porches, verandas, towers, and pergolas had been enclosed or removed years ago. I suddenly realized that the hotel I saw across the street didn't look anything like the place where I had tea with Clara. The porch always seemed open and inviting, with fresh paint and comfortable chairs scattered around. It was a place to watch the world go by and to be seen. It looked so different from this view.

Clara went on, "The Sunset had been designed to be a place for people who wanted something more, and from the beginning they made every effort to distinguish it from other hotels. This was the first 'a la carte' hotel in St. Petersburg. At that time hotels included meals in the seasonal rate, so guests always ate in the dining room of the place where they were staying. Those who wanted to dine someplace else could, but it meant they paid for the meal twice. At an 'a la carte' hotel meals did not have to be included in the seasonal rate. Guests who did not add meals could eat anywhere they chose. That gave them freedom and flexibility. If meals were not included by residents at the Sunset they could still eat here anytime; they just paid for the meal like they would at any restaurant.

"The 'a la carte' arrangement turned out to be perfect for Thomas and Adeline. If she felt well she would eat in the dining room or go into town for lunch or dinner. On days when she didn't feel well the nurse fixed meals in their apartment. Thomas dined with her when he could, but he often had meals on his own. Adeline kept to fairly scheduled mealtimes. Thomas, with his work, never knew when he might get a chance to eat. There was nothing regular about his schedule.

"When Adeline felt well, Thomas might spend free time attending a Phillies game, playing golf, fishing, or sailing. The dining room conveniently stayed open until 11 p.m. so he didn't have to rush back to eat.

"Adeline stayed busy that winter, but she preferred activities that were more sedentary than the ones Thomas enjoyed. On days when her energy levels were low she rested, sewed, or read. The nurse could take her to the park where she would sit in the sunshine, watch the activities on the Bay, and breathe in the clean, healing air. When she felt well, Adeline played croquet, shuffleboard, walked by the water, sailed, swam, or visited with Mrs. Grigg and the other guests. She loved bridge, and being an excellent player she played as often as she could. She also liked to entertain and often had guests for tea.

"It cost five cents to take the Davista trolley into town, and Adeline liked to ride into St. Petersburg to attend lectures or go shopping. She even took some golf lessons, though I heard she never played well. Being at the Sunset turned out to be just what she needed, and Adeline felt much better when they returned to Philadelphia at the end of season.

"Thomas and Adeline came back the following winter, but everything had changed. Their good friends, the Griggs, were gone. The United States had joined allies Britain and France in fighting the Great War, and Robert Grigg had enlisted in the service. His wife had returned to Philadelphia to be with her family while her husband fought in France. The new managers didn't open the hotel until just before Christmas. Thomas and Adeline arrived shortly after opening, but unfortunately her health was deteriorating quickly. This time the warmth, sunshine, and camaraderie of the other guests could not make a difference. Adeline passed away the following summer.

"Things changed for the hotel, too. The Fullers, having run into financial difficulties when the war continued longer than they expected, had second thoughts about owing a hotel. It took more time and money than they wanted to invest, so they decided to get out of the hotel business. The Sunset was sold for thirty thousand dollars."

I sat quietly, thinking about Adeline. I asked if she had ever come back to the hotel. Clara nodded, "Yes, she's here. We have become good friends over the years. She wanted to tell you her story but for some reason you can't see her. That is a shame; I am sure you would like her. She finds her invisibility to you very frustrating. She kept hoping that would change, but since it hasn't she asked me to share her story with you.

"I suggested coming to the park so I could tell the story without Adeline being around. She interrupts and wants me to add details that I don't feel are important. She hates it when I say she was a picky eater, not good at golf, liked to be pampered, and enjoyed being the center of attention—even though it is all true."

Adeline seemed to be an intriguing person. I asked Clara to tell me more about her. Hesitating for a bit she said, "She was much older than I, at least ten years. Everyone found her very attractive. She enjoyed being around people and had the ability to make each person feel like they were her best friend. She died at the age of thirty-five, and the last year of her life was very difficult."

I had a feeling I would have liked Adeline. I wondered if perhaps Clara might be a tiny bit jealous of her. I saw I needed to start home soon because the sea fog had begun to roll in again. As I rose to leave, I glimpsed through the fog a beautiful, well-dressed, young woman standing near a tree watching us. She smiled at me, winked, and then faded away. I knew Adeline's wish had come true; I had finally been able to see her.

Chocolate is nature's way for making up for Mondays.

HOT CHOCOLATE WITH PEPPERMINT SCHNAPPS

1½ cups of whole milk	½ cup of heavy cream
2 tsp. powdered sugar	½ tsp. espresso powder

8 oz. bittersweet chocolate (72% or higher) chopped
3-4 oz. of peppermint schnapps

In a medium sauce pan over medium heat whisk together milk, cream, powdered sugar and espresso powder until small bubbles appear around the edges. DO NOT let boil. Remove the pan from heat and stir in the chopped chocolate until melted. Return to low heat if needed for the mixture to melt. Total cooking time should take about five minutes.

When chocolate has melted and is ready to serve, pour in the schnapps and stir.

Serve with lots of whipped cream and a peppermint stick. This is a rich, thick drink and the whipped cream may be used to thin it.

Makes two large cups.

The popular green benches in 1925

The best teachers are those who show you where to look but don't tell you what to see.

ALEXANDRA L. TRENFOR

The Fultons

My daily walks now went by the Sunset Hotel, and Clara always had tea waiting for me. We fell into the habit of sitting on the porch and talking until we had gone through two pots of tea, which some days took longer than others. I enjoyed the time we spent together, and I knew Clara did too. She always had something interesting to tell me about the history of the area. So I have to admit it was a surprise to see her, stylishly dressed, waiting for me on the sidewalk. She wore an attractive silk blouse, wide legged wool slacks which she referred to as trousers, a long, flowing, loose jacket, a wide brimmed hat, and a beautiful pair of very high heels. She said she needed to go to the Jungle Hotel and asked if I would mind walking with her.

The Jungle Hotel was about a mile away. I looked at Clara. I couldn't imagine anyone walking a block in those shoes, let alone a mile. I asked if she would like to put on another pair of shoes that might be more comfortable. Huffily, she replied those were her favorite shoes and they were very comfortable. I knew nothing I could say would change her mind, so we started down the street.

Clara set a fairly slow pace giving us plenty of time to talk. I asked her how and when she started coming to St. Petersburg. Clara smiled, "Thomas loved this area and the Sunset Hotel, but after Adeline died he didn't want to come back alone. We married in the fall of 1920, about two years after Adeline's passing. Thomas asked me what I thought about coming to Florida for the winter. He didn't have to ask twice. He gave me a choice of several places we could stay, but I knew how much he loved the Sunset so that's where I chose.

"The hotel had recently been sold again, and opening day wouldn't be until right before Christmas. We decided to stay in Philadelphia for the holidays and come down after the first of the year. Thomas heard they were making several renovations to the hotel and he had concerns about how well it had been maintained. He wrote to Walter P. for information. Walter P. assured Thomas that he would find the Sunset up to date and with many more conveniences. He confidently stated we would like the hotel and the new managers, Robert Fulton and his wife. Walter P. said the Fultons had owned and operated several resorts and hotels around the country. They would manage the Sunset through the winter season and during the summer go to Winona Lake, Indiana, to run a resort there.

"I fell in love with the Sunset the first time I saw it. I felt at home immediately, and I still do." Clara paused for a moment, "When I started coming to the Sunset I was much younger than all of the other women. Luckily, some of the guests had daughters or granddaughters close to my age who would come to visit. That always made it more fun for me."

I looked at Clara closely. I had never been able to figure out how old she was, but she always seemed at least middle-aged to me. I wondered how old the people were who came to the hotel, especially if Clara and some of their granddaughters were the same age!

Forgetting that Clara could read my thoughts often caused me embarrassment. Looking highly annoyed she said tersely, "I was only twenty-seven when I first came!" I wisely let the remark pass without comment and waited patiently for her to continue. Fortunately, it didn't take long.

"As I said, I loved it here from the beginning. We had a beautiful apartment at the opposite end of the building from where Thomas and Adeline had stayed. It looked out over Central Avenue and had views of Sunset Park and Boca Ciega Bay. Our unit had a living room, a kitchen and eating area, a large bedroom with a dressing room, and a second smaller bedroom which Thomas used as an office.

"I never remember being bored or lonely during my time here. I stayed much too busy! There were always friends to meet and things to do. I swam, went boating or horseback riding, and even played a little golf. I went on outings, played cards and lawn sports, found new people to talk to, and of course, attended baseball games.

"The Fultons had a full entertainment schedule for the hotel. They planned events several times a month with speakers, musicians, and plays. I looked forward to afternoon teas where I could visit with the other guests and relax. The older women always included me in their activities. We would talk, sew, play bridge, or we might ride the trolley into St. Petersburg for shopping or lunch.

"Anytime we went into St. Petersburg we always sat on the green benches. I miss those green benches! You never knew who you might sit next to or where they might be from. It was a great way to meet people. The benches were a symbol of the city's friendliness. They were always full and you often had to wait for someone to get up before you could sit down. Let me tell you, some of those people could sit and talk for a very long time!

"Thomas and I enjoyed spending time together. We attended lectures and plays, went dancing in the evening at one of the clubs, had fresh seafood dinners with friends, went to ballgames, or took a boat out for a sail. Later, when we got a car, the staff would pack us a wonderful picnic in chaffing dishes, and we would take off to explore new places."

Clara stopped for a moment and shook her foot. I had a feeling her shoes might be hurting, but she didn't complain and gamely continued walking.

"The new managers kept busy running two hotels. Season here went from December to the end of March, and season at the Winona Hotel in Indiana ran from the end of May until the first of September. Management of the two hotels was very different. People did go to Winona Lake for the entire summer, but most people went only for a couple of weeks to attend one of the chautauquas. Winona Lake was the home of the famous evangelist Billy Sunday, and hundreds of thousands of people came each summer to hear him preach."

Chautauquas! What in the world were those? I remember somewhere hearing the name Billy Sunday, but I knew nothing about him. I couldn't imagine why thousands of people would want to hear him speak. Clara obviously had been exaggerating about the hundreds of thousands part.

Clara looked at me. "I forget how young you really are. Chautauquas were very popular from the late 1800's until about 1930. The best way I know to describe them is that they were like a summer camp for adults. Speakers, musicians, entertainers, preachers, and specialists came from all over the country, and for two weeks people would take classes, learn new ideas, hear sermons, attend lectures and go to concerts. Teddy Roosevelt called chautauquas 'the most American thing in America.'

"Billy Sunday was a world-renowned evangelist. His family had been so poor that as a young child he had been sent to an orphanage to live. Being a natural athlete he used his talent to escape poverty. He excelled at baseball and signed with the Chicago White Stockings to play center field. He had an ability to steal bases that fans loved. In 1892, he earned over four hundred dollars a month playing ball. That equaled what the average person earned in a year! Fans were shocked when he quit baseball to become a minister with the Chicago YMCA. His salary dropped to almost nothing and his name disappeared from the news.

"Everyone thought he had made a horrible mistake, but he proved them wrong. It turned out he was a much better preacher than baseball player. Within a few years his revival services were attended by tens of thousands of people a week in cities like Philadelphia, Baltimore, and New York. Over a hundred million people heard him preach, and that was before television or your net had even been thought of!

"Billy Sunday and his wife eventually decided to settle at Winona Lake which was already a well-established resort and chautauqua. They built a huge tabernacle that seated thousands of people, and he filled it every time he spoke. The Fultons told us that over two hundred and fifty thousand people a summer would come to the chautauquas at the Lake. The majority of them came because they wanted a chance to hear Billy Sunday preach."

Clara had slowed down considerably and seemed to be limping slightly. She stopped, bent down to rub one of her feet, and asked how much farther it was. I hated to tell her we had only gone a couple of blocks and had several more to go. Clara sighed, "I guess I didn't realize it was so far. I think I will go back to the hotel and catch the trolley."

She brightened when she saw a couple walking toward us on the other side of the street. "Oh, there are the Fultons! I'll walk back with them." Without even saying goodbye she hurried across the street and joined the couple headed back toward the Sunset.

I finished my walk alone.

Walter P. Fuller

Yesterday was interesting, today is important,
tomorrow is exciting.
With that formula you can live quite a long time if you don't
get run over by a truck.

WALTER P. FULLER

Walter P. Fuller

"Walter P. is upset with me," Clara said when we met again. "He says I've spent all this time telling you about other people when he's the interesting one. He says I need to get on to the good stuff." She laughed delightedly, "He is right, you can't tell the story of this area without talking about him.

"The problem is I hardly know where to start. Walter P., like his father, was a businessman, but he was much more adventuresome and open to trying new things. While he liked to talk about his father losing fortunes, Walter P. lost his share of fortunes, too. He loved a challenge and took on anything that came along. He founded the first Boy Scout troop in St. Petersburg and became the first paid football coach at the high school. He worked as a reporter and an editor at the St. Petersburg Times. He got into politics and served in the state legislature and as a Democratic state committeeman. He was responsible for several other firsts in St, Petersburg, including a golf course, a shopping mall, and a nightclub. He also built two hotels, a country club, an airport, and over one thousand homes. He wasn't afraid of failure and he had a story about everything he did.

"Things were going well for him in 1916. Construction had started on the Sunset Hotel and the golf course had just opened. While most golfers today would consider it a fairly easy course, we found it challenging. We were all just learning to play the game. That course had everything, including alligators. We thought it was swell!

"For some reason the area around the hotel had been slow to develop. There were only three homes in the vicinity when Walter P. decided to build his own house just a few blocks down Park Street. He chose a two and a half acre lot with a spectacular view of Boca Ciega Bay. Walter P. liked to tell how his friend sketched out plans for the house on a cypress roofing shingle as he described the home he wanted. Like many of Walter P.'s memories, it may or may not have happened that way, but it made a good story, and to him that held more importance than a factual story."

Clara looked out over the water and asked if I knew what Boca Ciega meant. I had no idea. I had never even thought about it meaning anything. It was just the name of the Bay.

"Well, I wondered about it so I asked Thomas. He said it is Spanish for 'hidden mouth.' I think the name is much prettier in Spanish than English, don't you? It is such a long bay that I can understand why it got the name."

I didn't want Clara going off on a tangent about the name of a body of water. I wanted to know about something much more important. "Tell me about Walter P.'s house! Is it still here? Does anyone live in it? Can I see it? Where is it?"

Clara looked at me in surprise. "Yes, the house is at 424 Park Street and someone does live there. I don't suppose many people today know or care that Walter P. once owned the house. It has had several owners since his time. There's a tall wall around the property now, and the house sits toward the back of the lot. The front gardens are about all you can see from the street.

"The fact that there is a house there at all is a story of its own. Walter P. had the lumber for the home cut from a forest between where Gulfport is now and Boca Ciega Bay. He hired builders with the agreement that they would work ten-hour days. They would be paid half in cash at sixty cents an hour, and half in land. The arrangement pleased everyone.

"Shortly after construction started the Fullers' fortunes began to collapse. Even though he couldn't pay the workers for five months Walter P. convinced the men to finish the house. He gave his word that they would be paid every cent they were owed. Unfortunately, things kept getting worse and the Fullers went into bankruptcy. To Walter P.'s dismay the liquidators refused to honor his agreement with the workmen. He had given his word that the men would be paid and they had trusted him. He vowed he would keep his promise to the workers.

"Walter P. tried everything he could think of, but he could not find a way to get the money needed for the men's back wages. Finally, he went to a friend and explained the situation. He didn't want money for himself or his family; he only wanted a loan to pay the workers what they were owed. In return he would hand over the deed to his new house. His friend wrote him a check for seven thousand dollars, and Walter P. was able to pay his employees all their back wages. It took a couple years but he did regain the deed to his home and got back on his feet."

I asked Clara to tell me about the house. "It's a two-story brick home with lots of windows and beautiful woodwork. There's a lovely walnut staircase in the entry way and the rooms are large and comfortable. We went to some great parties there, but to be honest the inside of the house wasn't where we spent our time. We were outside around the pool, in the gardens, or by the dock enjoying the beautiful view."

Clara suddenly gasped that she would be late. She said she would see me soon and disappeared inside the hotel. I didn't know what to do. I waited for a few minutes, and when she did not reappear I decided that I might as well continue my walk. I definitely planned to go past the Fuller house.

As I neared the house I could tell someone was having a party. I heard music, laughter, and voices. Arriving at the address I found a tall brick wall, just as Clara had mentioned. I could see little from the street except for the hint of well-kept gardens and the roofline of the house. The party was definitely here, and it sounded like a lot of people had been invited.

I heard my name being called and looked around. Clara stood inside the gate waving at me. I could hardly believe my eyes when I saw her. She looked so young! She had on a sleeveless dress that stopped above her knees. It appeared to be made of black fringe. Around her neck hung a long string of knotted pearls that fell almost to her knees. Her hair was bobbed and she wore a pair of heels that were at least three inches tall. She held a martini glass in one hand, and I'd swear she was chewing gum. "Do you like it?" she asked as she spun around. With every move she made the entire dress swayed.

I stared. She looked good in that dress! She was every inch a flapper. I wouldn't have been surprised to hear her say "not to take any wooden nickels" or that the party was "the bee's knees." I could see Clara was enjoying herself.

She motioned for me to come closer and began pulling on the gate impatiently. "Rats! I hoped I would be able to open this and let you in. I know you want to see the house. It is a swell party and everybody's here!" She gave one more hard yank on the gate and then gave up. Looking at me mischievously she said, "I have to go back to the party now, it's the bee's knees!" As she started back down the driveway she turned and looked back over her shoulder. "I'll see you soon. Don't take any wooden nickels, kiddo!"

Watching her dance down the driveway I knew that could not have been her first martini. I longed to be at that party, but with my sweats and trainers I knew I would have been out of place. The music and the voices were fading. I couldn't keep standing there staring in the gate or someone would call the police. I continued with my walk, knowing without a doubt I had missed a great party!

Walter P. Fuller's House in the 1920s

Photo from St. Petersburg Museum of History

Instead of giving money to found colleges to promote learn-
ing, why don't we pass a constitutional amendment prohibit-
ing anybody from learning anything? If it works as good as
the Prohibition one did, why, in five years we would have the
smartest race of people on the earth.

WILL ROGERS

Prohibition

The next day I found Clara sitting on the porch of the hotel, and she didn't look well. She wore a wide brimmed hat which blocked the light from her eyes. She motioned for me to join her and told me to walk as quietly as possible. I noticed she had black coffee in her cup instead of the tea she usually drank. She said she had a headache and needed to rest for a while.

The Clara sitting across from me was a more mature version of the girl I had seen the afternoon before. She did not offer me a cup of coffee, so I poured my own. I added a spoonful of sugar and began to stir. The spoon inadvertently hit the side of the cup and Clara winced. I quickly asked about the party. Grimacing and smiling at the same time she replied, "It was swell." She told me she wished I could have been there. I sat quietly, waiting to hear about the party, but Clara took the conversation in an unexpected direction.

"I rarely drank before Prohibition, just a glass of wine on rare occasions," she said in a very soft voice. "Few women did. I don't know why we started drinking so much during Prohibition, but I think speakeasies had a lot to do with it. They became our main sources for entertainment, and we went to them to drink and have fun."

Clara paused and took another sip of her coffee. "Tampa Bay and Miami were the two big tourist destinations in Florida during the 1920s and '30s. Local officials in both places pretty much ignored Prohibition. The areas were dependent on tourists as their main source of income. People came here to vacation and to have a good time, which meant they expected to be able to have a drink now and then. If they couldn't get liquor here they could get on a boat and in a few hours be in Cuba or the Bahamas, where alcohol was legal. No one wanted the tourists and their money going out of the country, so certain things were just ignored.

"When Prohibition began in January of 1920, we weren't worried; everyone thought the law would be repealed quickly. We found it great fun to go out before Prohibition started and purchase cases of liquor to have on hand. We bought what we thought we would need for a year. No one expected it to last thirteen years!

"At first it was a game as we tried to hide our bottles. Even the Sunset had a secret room where liquor could be stored out of sight. We all knew we were breaking the law, and we had fun seeing if we could do it without being caught. That got old fast!

"Most of us thought we were well stocked, but we soon found that we were drinking more than expected and our supplies dwindled quickly. When we ran out of liquor a bootlegger or a speakeasy were the only recourses we had. Both were illegal, but so was having a drink. Many of us became habitual law breakers.

"At the start of Prohibition Walter P. didn't drink, but he had no problem if other people did. A shortage of alcohol never seemed to be a problem at his parties. He always knew someone who could provide anything needed for a good time.

"One of my favorite memories from that time involved Thomas and Walter P. We still laugh about what happened. The prelude to the adventure had actually taken place several years earlier when Walter P. was living on Park Street. A boat moored at his dock, and the captain asked if he would be interested in buying a load of coconut palms trees for his real estate developments.

"Walter P. had no interest in the offering until the man mentioned that he also had one hundred cases of liquor on the boat. The captain wanted everything off his boat before nightfall because he was concerned about being hijacked or caught by the Feds.

"So much liquor was being smuggled into this area that hijackers regularly roamed the waters around here. Anyone they caught with a boatload of booze would lose their cargo, their boat, and on more than one occasion their life. Being caught by federal agents had no better consequences. When they intercepted you, you lost your boat, your cargo, and your freedom. If you were stopped with a boatload of liquor you would not come out a winner.

"After a great deal of haggling, Walter P. wrote a check and officially became a bootlegger. He had the liquor carried into the house and locked in a small, unused room. I know you've heard the saying 'out of sight, out of mind.' Well, because Walter P. didn't drink at the time, that's what happened. The contents of the closet were forgotten. Two years later he sold the house with the unremembered cases of liquor still locked in the room. The people who bought the house didn't move in right away, and the house sat empty with its secret hidden inside.

"That's when Thomas came into the story. He was working with Walter P. and stopped by one evening to talk about new construction in the Jungle development. When they finished their discussion, Thomas asked Walter P. if he had anything to drink. Walter P. was no longer abstaining, and for some reason he suddenly remembered the cases in the locked room at his old house. He told Thomas about them and said he wondered if they were still there. They decided they needed to go over and see what had happened to the liquor.

"After it got dark, the two of them snuck over and broke into the empty house. They discovered that the room where the cases had been left was still locked. Walter P. unlocked the door and there were all one hundred cases! He and Thomas quickly decided it would not be wise to let something that valuable sit in an empty house, wasting away. Someone needed to rescue the cases, and they felt up to the challenge. They found an old wheelbarrow and together they moved the liquor, one case at a time, from Walter P.'s old house to his new one. Luckily, there were only a few homes in the area or they never could have pulled it off. It took them all night, and more than one case had to be opened and sampled as the move went on."

Clara paused, refreshed her cup of coffee, and took a sip. "For his help, Thomas got his drink and a case as well. We felt like we had been given a bar of gold. We vowed to make that case last as long as we could, but we failed miserably." Clara gave a little chuckle, "I'm sure the people who bought Walter P.'s home never had a clue about the treasure that had been removed from the house."

Clara seemed to be reviving a bit and was starting to look more like herself. I asked if she thought going for a walk would help her feel better. She gave me a look that let me know she did not think much of my idea. The wind suddenly seemed to pick up because a couple of the chairs on the porch moved with a scraping sound. Somewhere in the distance I heard someone singing, badly off key. I looked around to see if I could tell where the noise came from. When I turned back to Clara I could tell she was angry.

"They are doing that on purpose because they didn't get invited to Walter P.'s party!" she hissed. "Come on!" She grabbed my hand and stood up. "Let's take that walk after all! It will be more relaxing than staying here."

One of the many Tent Cities in the Tampa Bay area

Photo Courtesy, Tampa-Hillsborough County Public Library System

We travel not to escape life, but for life not to escape us.

ANONYMOUS

Tent City

When I arrived at the hotel I saw Clara sitting on the porch having tea. A woman sat across from her and they seemed to be enjoying each other's company. I hesitantly went up to join them. I had come to feel that Clara belonged to me, and I have to admit I felt a little resentful about sharing her.

Clara saw me and smiled. "Come join us. I want you to meet a good friend of mine, Marie Owens. I met Marie and her husband, Joseph, not long after I started coming down here. We've been friends ever since. We were talking about the modifications they made to the hotel back in the twenties. One of the best changes happened in 1923, when they enlarged the dining room and got the new chef. While the food had always been good, it became something extraordinary. People came from all around the area to eat at the Sunset."

I sat down and looked at the table expecting the usual tea and cookies. Instead, the table was filled with beautiful sandwiches and cakes.

"Marie doesn't live here anymore, but this is where we met. She often comes to visit me. We used to have lunch together every day. We looked forward to seeing what would be on the menu and just being with one another."

I began to relax when I realized that Marie would not be a threat to my friendship with Clara but an addition to it. However, I was puzzled and asked why I could see Marie so easily when I couldn't see others, like Adeline or Walter P.

Marie smiled, "I guess it's like you and Clara; for some reason we are just compatible. You and I have seen and talked to each other several times since you moved into the area."

Had I seen her before? I looked at her closely and realized that there was something familiar about her.

"I spoke with you yesterday when you were walking by the old Jungle Hotel. We talked about how happy we were that the weather had finally started warming up."

I stared at her in amazement. I did know her! We had spoken several times. I thought she lived in the neighborhood. I never dreamed that she was, as Clara calls it, "in another dimension."

Clara smiled at her friend, "Marie and her husband came to the Sunset for the first time in 1923. We quickly became friends because we were both about the same age. I want her to tell you how she got to the Sunset. Did you ever hear of the Tin Can Tourists?"

I shook my head no. I had no idea what she meant by Tin Can Tourists. Clara's smile grew bigger, "Good! I want Marie to tell you all about them."

Marie set her cup down and looked at me, "I guess the best place to start is a few years before I met Clara. I was living in Chicago and training to be a nurse. During that time I met a handsome young man studying to be a doctor. We fell in love and planned to get married as soon as we both graduated. Then the Great War started. When the United States entered the war in 1917, Joseph enlisted in the service and served as a medic. When he came home, he finished his training and we were married.

Marie hesitated for a moment, looking at a little red convertible stopped at the traffic light in front of the hotel. She seemed to get sidetracked by the car. "Americans fell in love with the automobile right from the beginning. At first they were so expensive they could only be afforded by the very rich, but Henry Ford believed everyone should be able to own a car. He built the Model T and started mass producing it. By 1923, the cost of a new Model T Ford had dropped from eight hundred and twenty-five dollars down to three hundred and fifty-five dollars. That meant the average person could own an automobile, and everybody wanted one. They sold over fifteen million Model Ts!

"Our parents gave us one for a wedding present and we decided to travel before Joseph started his practice. In the early years of the automobile, driving was a challenge because roads were designed for horses and wagons, not cars. However, as millions of people got automobiles that changed. Roads for motor vehicles were being built all across the United States.

"People loved the freedom of the automobile. You could make your own schedule and go where you wanted to go. Once you bought a car the major cost for travel was the gasoline. Oil companies tried to get the price of gas raised to twenty-five cents a gallon, but people protested so much that the price dropped back to sixteen cents a gallon."

The stop light changed and the little red car drove off. Marie's eyes followed it down the street as she continued, "We weren't sure where we wanted to go on our trip. Some of our friends had driven down to Florida a couple of years earlier, and they suggested we do that. We could get on Highway 41 right there in Chicago and follow it all the way to Miami. We were excited about the idea of seeing some of the United States, so we decided to take Highway 41 and see where it led us.

"Cars weren't too reliable in those early days. You needed to know how to make minor repairs because you never knew where, or when, your car might break down. A flat tire was a normal part of driving so anyone who drove had to be able to change a tire. The top speed on our Model T was forty miles an hour. If we went a hundred and twenty-five miles in a day, we thought we had made good time.

"Any trip that took more than a day required special preparations. You knew you might not be able to find a cafe or a place to spend the night, so you had to pack a tent, cots, bedding, cooking utensils, and plenty of food.

"Joseph and I eagerly started out. When we heard about something that sounded interesting we stopped and stayed as long as we wanted. We had everything we needed, and as long as the weather stayed nice we enjoyed traveling.

"Our friends had ended their trip in St. Petersburg, and they said we should stop here for a while. When we arrived we found the weather perfect and the people friendly. It had been a long trip, so we decided to spend the rest of the winter here.

"The influx of tourists had become a problem all over Florida, and St. Petersburg was no exception. Travel had been so expensive before the automobile that only the rich could afford it, so visitors had been limited. The Model T changed that. Suddenly large numbers of people were coming to Florida, but they weren't the type of visitors that Floridians were used to having. They were younger, middle-class, and adventurers. They had their own cars, so many of them didn't stay in one place all season; they liked to move around.

"When our friends had arrived in St. Petersburg they couldn't find a hotel anywhere, but they heard about a Tent City that had just opened. They went to look at it. To their surprise they found it was free to stay there, so they signed up for a space. They were lucky they arrived when they did because all one hundred and twenty-five camp spaces were filled within a few days.

"They had a wonderful time that winter. They met young people wanting to see what life was like outside of their hometown and veterans who were trying to forget the horrors of war. There were retirees hoping to escape the cold northern winters, and people with seasonal jobs, like farmers and entertainers in the summer resorts, who just wanted to relax in the warmth and sunshine. No one was poor. Many would have preferred to stay in a hotel, but there were none available. The people in Tent City bonded quickly because they all had a common interest, the desire to experience new things."

Clara had shown remarkable restraint by not saying anything for a long time, but she'd reached her limit. "I remember Tent City," she said. "The mayor, Noel Mitchell, didn't know what to do with all the people who arrived that year. He had to do something quickly, so like many other mayors in Florida, he created a Tent City. The City had garbage collection, toilet facilities, and clean hot and cold water. Towns all over Florida were doing what they could to make the surge of tourists feel at home. Tampa even allowed the children living in their Tent City to attend school for fifty cents a week."

Marie smiled and reminded Clara that this was her story. Clara apologized and Marie continued, "Locals called these new types of travelers Tin Can Tourists. The name came from their arriving in Model T's, which were called Tin Lizzies, and because they brought along boxes of food in tin cans.

"The Tent City residents in Tampa decided to band together to make sure that the people in the camp were safe and had wholesome entertainment. They formed the first Tin Can Club, and the idea spread quickly. Membership in a Tin Can Club was very simple. You had to apply in person, be at least twelve years old, and live in the camp. You had to learn the secret handshake and the official theme song, 'The More We Get Together.' Everyone wanted to join!"

Clara interrupted, "Members of the Club here had so much fun that I would have joined myself if I could have. They had dances, card games, and shuffleboard tournaments. Their evenings were filled with storytelling, lectures, plays, and music.

"At first, people here supported the idea of a Tent City, but locals quickly found these tourists were different from the ones who had been coming for so many years. They fixed their own meals instead of eating in restaurants. Not only that but they weren't paying for accommodations. They provided their own entertainment--shows, lectures, classes, dances, concerts--and that didn't cost them anything either. Sentiment quickly began to turn against the residents of Tent City, because locals realized they were having fun down here for free! A demand went up for Tent City to be closed.

Clara sighed, "People had very different views about the Tin Canners. The women at the Sunset talked about them as though they were the lowest form of life. I saw them as people who were having fun, and I was a little envious of all the young people at the City. Others like Walter P. saw them as an opportunity. He realized many of them liked the area enough that they were thinking about moving here. He sold land to quite a few of them."

Marie nodded and took over the story again. "Resentment grew. Locals started using the term 'Tin Can Tourist' with scorn. They sneered that these were people who came down with one shirt and a twenty dollar bill, and neither one was changed while they were here. However, people in Tent City wore the name as a badge of pride and ignored the taunts.

"Tent City was closed after the first year, but several private camp grounds were set up the following years. We knew where people from Chicago stayed, so we reserved a spot there. We had a great time when we got here."

Clara looked at her and started laughing. For a moment Marie looked a little embarrassed, but she too began to laugh. "Okay, to be truthful we weren't really camping people. The fun wore off quickly. I wanted a place with a real bed, a bathroom not shared by a camp, and I hated having to cook every meal.

"Finding a hotel anywhere in Florida was impossible. We were talking about returning home when I overheard a woman saying she didn't know what to do about her elderly aunt at the Sunset Hotel. The couple she traveled with had a family emergency and needed to return to Chicago immediately. The aunt required both a nurse and a chauffeur. She could not stay here alone, but she refused to go home.

"I told Joseph about the conversation. We agreed it sounded like the perfect way to keep us out of the cold Chicago winter. We introduced ourselves to the woman and told her we had heard about her dilemma. I explained I had a nursing degree and my husband could drive; we asked if we could help. After talking with us, and getting our assurance we could be here for the rest of season, she asked if we would meet her aunt.

"We called on Miss Minnie the next afternoon. The three of us liked each other immediately. We learned our pay would include a room and meals here at the Sunset! We accepted the job, went back to the camp, packed the things we would need going home, and gave everything else away. Then we moved into the Sunset Hotel."

"You cannot believe my excitement when I heard Marie had moved in as a nurse for one of the guests!" Clara said. "Finally, there was someone else my age at the Sunset."

Marie patted Clara on the arm, "I don't know what I would have done without you. No one could have been kinder than Miss Minnie, but she was very old and frail. She liked getting out when she could; however, she spent most of the time in her room or around the hotel. Having you here made my stay much more enjoyable."

Turning back to me she continued, "Thomas and Joseph got along well. Thomas introduced my husband to Walter P. Of course, he took Joseph over to the Jungle to look at land. I knew the minute they came back that we would be buying a lot there.

"It took us a while to save up the money for the house we wanted, but we returned each year for at least part of season. We always stayed at the Sunset until the year we began building our house. Then we moved to the Jungle Hotel, because it was closer to our lot. That made it easier for Joseph to watch the construction. I enjoyed the Jungle, but I missed the Sunset and Clara."

The two women obviously had a strong bond. I suspected they had a lot they wanted to talk about, so I thanked Marie for sharing her story and said I needed to go.

Reaching the street I looked back. I couldn't see them anymore, but I could hear them laughing. I knew they had been blessed to have had so many years of friendship.

Think what a better world it would be if we all, the whole world, had cookies and milk about three o'clock every afternoon and then lay down on our blankets for a nap.

Barbara Jordan

SOFT GINGER SNAP COOKIES

¾ cup butter softened	1cup sugar
1 large egg	¼ cup molasses
2¼ cups of all-purpose flour	2 tsp. ground ginger
1 tsp. baking soda	¾ tsp. ground cinnamon
¾ tsp. ground cloves	¼ tsp. salt

½ cup chopped pecans (or more if you like)
Pre-heat oven to 350°

Cream butter and sugar until light and fluffy. Beat in egg and molasses.

Add dry ingredients to the batter. After mixing well stir in pecans.

Let batter sit for a few minutes, it will be easier to work with. Form batter into small balls (1-1½ inches) and immediately roll in a plate of sugar. Place two inches apart on an ungreased baking sheet. Bake for 10-12 minutes until puffy and lightly browned.

Remove to a wire rack to cool. Yields 2-2 ½ dozen cookies.

The Jungle area in St. Petersburg

Photo from St. Petersburg Museum of History

Tocobaga Indian

*The tragedy of life is not death, but what we let die inside us
while we live.*

NATIVE AMERICAN QUOTE

Tocobaga

Clara and I had become exercise buddies. Luckily somewhere she had been able to find a sturdy pair of shoes so we could now enjoy our outings. Today we had decided to make the mile-and-a-half trip down Park Street to Elbow Lane. As we set off, Clara asked me where I liked to walk. I told her my favorite routes went along the water. I enjoyed the beauty and peacefulness there. She said she liked going down Park Street because it brought back so many wonderful memories.

I wondered if Clara ever felt uneasy when she walked by the Indian Sacred Grounds on Park Street. I often did. I told her how I felt and waited for her to tell me I needed to stop letting my imagination run wild. After a moment she said, "I think that's probably normal. I, too, sometimes feel sadness there. That site has seen so much heartbreak and so many lives destroyed. I would be surprised if you didn't feel that way."

I looked at her in shock. That was not like Clara!

She continued, "Native people inhabited this area for thousands of years. The last group, the Tocobaga, spent their days fishing, hunting, and farming. They usually lived peacefully, but it wasn't unheard of for them to go to war. When they did they could be cruel conquerors. They considered torture and enslaving their enemies a natural part of war.

"After Columbus 'discovered' the New World, others quickly followed. The first explorations were led by the Spanish, who arrived on the west coast of Florida in the early 1500s. Unfortunately, they weren't as interested in exploring the new land as they were in claiming any gold or treasures they might find.

"The arrival of the Spanish meant the end for the people who lived here. The natives lost their land, their homes, and their lives because of the invaders. Almost every trace of their civilization has been destroyed; it is as if they never existed. Their spirits are saddened and angry about this, and I think they should be!"

We continued walking. I waited for Clara to go on with the story, but she seemed to be lost in her own thoughts. We were getting close to Elbow Lane when a feeling came over me that we were being followed. I felt very uneasy and told Clara I thought we should walk on as quickly as possible.

She demanded to know what had me so concerned. I whispered that I thought someone was following us. Just then the bushes near us rustled. It could have been the wind, but I didn't think so. Clara looked toward the bushes and then called, "Henry, come out here right now! You're scaring people."

No one appeared, but I could see some of the branches moving slightly. I told Clara I really thought we should go up to the park where there would be people.

"It's just Henry," she said impatiently. "I wish he would come out and talk to people when he wants something. After all, I am his friend!"

She stood patiently. As far as I could tell no one appeared. I heard another slight rustling in the bushes. Clara waited quietly for a moment or two and sighed. She turned to me, "I need to talk with Henry and it may take a few minutes. He is old and lonely. Sometimes he just needs a friend. You can either wait for me here or go on up to Elbow Lane." She walked into the shadows.

I had no idea who Henry was and I wasn't going to wait to find out. I called to Clara that I would walk on and left quickly. When I reached the parking lot by the restaurant I felt much more comfortable. There were people around and I relaxed as I looked out over Boca Ciega Bay.

A movement, off to the side and among the trees, caught my attention. I turned and glimpsed an unusual couple, standing arm in arm, looking out over the water. The girl, perhaps in her middle teens, had long dark hair and seemed to be wearing a deerskin dress. The young man with her appeared to be dressed as a Spanish conquistador. The girl, sensing my presence, turned and looked at me. She smiled and then they disappeared. The whole sighting took only a second or two. I shook my head. Had I really seen the couple or had I only imagined them after what Clara just told me?

I heard footsteps behind me and Clara came up. "I hoped you would get to meet Henry, but he was not receptive to the idea. The things that happened here took place a long time ago, but to Henry they seem like recent happenings.

"You see, when the Spanish came they brought more than a desire to conquer. They also brought diseases and illnesses that the people living here had no immunity against. Within a few years after the invaders arrival, all the natives in this area were gone. Because he was a Tocobaga, I suppose it is only natural that Henry is very wary of strangers. He doesn't seem to understand that since he's already dead nothing you have could hurt him."

I told Clara I was offended by her suggestion that I might have some horrible disease that would kill an innocent person. She chuckled, "Don't worry; no one would ever call Henry an innocent person."

Clara sighed, "There are so many stories about Henry, the Tocobaga, and the Spanish. They often contradict each other and finding out what is true is not easy. I want to tell you his story, but I need to warn you that it isn't pleasant.

"Henry's real name is Hirrihigua, but that's too hard to say, so I call him Henry. He was a chief, but among the Tocobaga being a chief meant more than being a leader. It also meant you were a god. Henry was said to have been a handsome man and a strong leader with the admiration of his village and many of the other tribes."

Clara and I walked out on the dock. We found an empty bench and sat down. I suddenly remembered the young couple I had seen and told Clara about them. I asked if she knew who they might be. She shook her head. Her voice held a puzzled tone when she told me she had never seen them.

After a few seconds, Clara went back to her story, "The King of Spain appointed a Spanish explorer, Pánfilo de Narváez, to be the governor of this part of the New World. In 1528, Narváez is supposed to have landed, right where we are sitting, with six hundred men and five ships. He claimed the area for Spain. What happened after their landing depends on who is telling the story. This version came from Henry. He's probably told it to his advantage, but modern historians seem to agree with his account.

"Narváez had a reputation as a very ruthless and cruel man, and he proudly lived up to it. He came on shore with about half his men and began to explore the area. He believed there was gold here and he intended to find it. After a search, which yielded no treasure, Narváez demanded a meeting with Henry. The chief was ordered to tell the invaders where to find gold.

"Henry couldn't tell them because there was no gold here. Narváez refused to believe it. He became so irate that he pulled out his sword and cut off the chief's nose. When Henry's mother saw what happened she ran to help her son. Narváez, infuriated that the woman would come to the aid of a savage, turned his dogs loose on her. They killed and ate her in front of the horrified village.

"As you can imagine, that did not go over well with the Tocobaga and surrounding tribes. Fierce battles broke out and many people were killed. Eventually, Narváez and his men escaped, and he continued his search for the gold he knew was here. However, instead of being met by obedient natives bearing treasure as he expected, everywhere he went angry warriors were lying in ambush, waiting for him.

"After countless battles, Narváez finally had to accept that he, and the few men he had left, needed to leave quickly or they would all be killed. They could not get back to their ships, so Narváez ordered his men to build rafts which they would use to sail across the Gulf to the safety of Mexico.

"Morale among the men was low. They had been told they would be conquerors in this new land, but instead they had lost almost every battle they had fought. Their visions of gold and wealth had vanished. They no longer had any faith or trust in their leader. The men had seen how cruel Narváez could be, and they knew he had little concern for those under him. His only interest lay in gaining wealth and power for himself.

"As the rafts were being built, the men discussed how they could all safely survive the trip. Because so many were sick or injured, there would have to be a careful division of the able-bodied men if everyone was to make it safely across the Gulf. Narváez, however, had no interest in seeing that his men survive the voyage. His only concern was in getting to safety himself. He selected every strong, able-bodied man for his raft and left the others to fend for themselves.

"Not long after setting sail they ran into violent storms. The men did not have the strength to fight the squalls. Only four members of the group survived the voyage and made it to Mexico. Narváez was not one of them. Oddly, none of the survivors had any idea what had happened to their captain, and none of them seemed to care."

Clara suddenly stood. "I just remembered something that might explain the couple you saw! I will be right back."

She disappeared for a few minutes and returned with a smile on her face, "I think Henry must be mellowing in his old age. He told me that he hoped he would be able to see the couple. He wants to give them his blessing.

"Henry has never said anything about this story, but I have a feeling it's true. Narváez had a young officer by the name of Juan Ortiz. Juan had taken off to do some exploring on his own when he suddenly found himself taken prisoner by the Tocobaga. The villagers, who had just seen their chief mutilated and his mother murdered, wanted revenge. They tortured Juan and were getting ready to burn him alive when Henry's oldest daughter, Princess Hirrihigua, intervened.

"She begged her father to spare the young man's life. The Princess had always been Henry's favorite child, and he found it hard to say no to her request. Juan received his freedom. However, the young woman knew her father would change his mind and come after the handsome young conquistador. Something more would have to be done to protect him.

"A marriage had been arranged between the Princess and a chief of a Mocoso tribe. The Mocoso and the Tocobaga were enemies, and it was hoped that the marriage would bring unity between the two tribes. Princess Hirrihigua went to her future husband and asked for his protection for the young Spaniard. He granted her request, perhaps more to anger Henry than as a kindness to her.

"Her action had disastrous effects! Henry felt betrayed by his daughter when he learned what had happened. In anger, he vowed never to speak to the princess again and banished her from the tribe. I don't know what happened to her after that. It is possible the marriage agreement fell apart and she had to leave the area. However, it is just as possible that the Mocoso insisted the marriage take place, just to spite her father.

"Juan lived with the Mocoso until Hernando De Soto and his men came through the area several years later. The Mocoso offered Juan his freedom, and he chose to go with the Spaniards. Juan, having learned several native dialects while he was a captive, served as De Soto's translator for the rest of the trip."

Clara sat quietly for a few minutes. When she spoke again the sorrow in her voice was obvious. "Princess Hirrihigua had to know her actions would anger her father, jeopardize her marriage, and perhaps even cost her life. It is hard to believe she would have given up so much to save Juan Ortiz if she hadn't cared for him. I hope they were the couple you saw and they have been able to find happiness together."

We sat looking out over the water. Clara had been right; there had been a lot of sadness here. As we rose to go I saw the young couple again, standing arm in arm. I knew Clara saw them, too. From among the shadows I saw an old man emerge. I heard Clara gasp, "Henry!" The couple must have heard her because they both turned. The old man walked slowly toward the young people. When he reached them he embraced the girl and then the young man. Princess Hirrihigua looked at me, smiled, and then all three were gone.

Clara and I stood waiting to see if anyone would reappear. No one did.

I heard Clara whisper, "Goodbye, Henry. I hope you have found companions who will travel with you. I hope the winds will blow your loneliness away and the tracks your moccasins leave from now on will be full of forgiveness and joy."

Hors D'oeuvre: A ham sandwich cut into forty pieces.

JACK BENNY

CREAM CHEESE AND GINGER SANDWICHES
Finely gate about 3 inches of fresh ginger
Softened cream cheese
½ cup of finely chopped pecans or walnuts
Watercress leaves

Trim the crusts off slices of bread. Mix the cream cheese with the grated ginger and chopped nuts. Spread the mixture on the bread. Place a single layer of fresh watercress leaves on one slice before closing the sandwich. Slice each sandwich into 4 long, thin strips. Garnish with watercress. Makes 12 sandwiches.

"Porch Teas" by Alice Bradley 1926 "Woman's Home Companion"

Jungle Prado in 1939

Photo from the State Archives of Florida

With the right music you either forget everything or you remember everything.

CALIMAR WHITE

Jungle Prado

A few days later I ran into Marie. We talked for a while and of course the conversation eventually led to Clara. Marie remarked that her friend knew so much about the area and had met almost everyone. Then she asked if I'd heard about the Gangplank and the tiger. I had no idea what she was talking about. Marie saw the puzzled expression on my face and laughed. "Ask Clara about it. It's a great story. You'll love it!" She waved good-bye and walked away.

I went to look for Clara. When I found her I told her I wanted to hear the story about the tiger walking the gangplank. Clara looked at me as if I had totally lost my mind. "I have no idea what in the world you are talking about! Where did you ever get that idea? I don't know anything about a tiger walking a gangplank."

Her reply surprised me. Marie seemed to be sure that I would enjoy hearing the story, but Clara acted as though she didn't know anything about it. I didn't think Marie had made it up, so I tried again. "Marie said to get you to tell me the story about the tiger and the gangplank."

Clara began to laugh, "Oh my!" she said, "Marie wasn't talking about the gangplank on a ship! She meant a speakeasy by the name of the Gangplank, and she wasn't talking about a real tiger either." Clara grinned, "Marie is right it's a great story, but to be absolutely correct I'd have to say it's several great stories.

"I guess where I should start is with the hurricane at the end of October in 1921. It came on shore between Clearwater and Tarpon Springs. Winds in the Davista area reached ninety miles an hour, and St. Petersburg had a ten to twelve foot storm surge on top of more than eight inches of rain.

"We were in Philadelphia and the first stories we heard about the hurricane horrified us. The news reports said Pass-a-Grille had been destroyed and one hundred and fifty people killed. As you can imagine, we were very worried. Thomas sent a wire to Walter P. immediately. His reply said news reports had greatly exaggerated the effects of the storm. We were assured that there had been little damage in the area.

"We later learned that Walter P. had modified the truth. He was correct that the first reports were exaggerated. Only three people had been killed, not one hundred and fifty, and while Pass-a-Grille had been hit hard it had not been destroyed. The damage in the area around the hotel was reported as minimal, but to be honest there were only a few things in this area: the hotel, a few houses, and the golf course.

"However, the destruction was much worse than Walter P. proclaimed. Most bridges in the area had either been destroyed or were severely damaged; large numbers of boats had been torn apart, and many trees had been uprooted. Roofs had been blown off buildings and churches, and scores of people lost their homes. Downtown St. Petersburg had been hit hard and all four of its piers were left in ruins.

"The official report about the hurricane stated that there had been no severe damage from the 'storm.' It had been decided that referring to it as a storm, rather than a hurricane, would lessen the effect on potential investors. Land sales had been going well. No one wanted anything to cause buyers hesitation about making a purchase. In the weeks leading up to season, men were hired to work around the clock to clean up and do repairs. The goal was for everything to appear as normal as possible when season started.

"Those of us who knew the area well saw few things out of the ordinary when we returned. There were some trees gone and many building had been freshly painted, but there was nothing unusual about that. The work had been done well and there were few signs of damage from the hurricane.

"We never found out what happened to the Sunset during the 'storm.' When we asked about damage to the hotel, people just smiled and said it wasn't too bad. The Sunset seemed fine when we arrived just before Christmas and activities proceeded as usual. Needless to say, we were surprised when we learned at the end of March that the hotel had been sold for just over one hundred thousand dollars. The new owners announced a long list of improvements they would be making once season ended. We knew that new owners usually made improvements after buying a hotel, but Thomas suspected some of the 'improvements' might have been necessitated by the hurricane.

"That same year Walter P. came down with what we jokingly called Jungle Fever. He had big ideas about what he wanted to do in the Jungle. He hoped to make the area so attractive that once people saw his offerings they wouldn't look anywhere else.

"The inspiration for one of his best ideas came from our trips to Havana. We made a couple of trips there each year. We all enjoyed Cuba with its warm weather, legal alcohol, great entertainment, and nightlife. We would gamble on the horses, go to baseball games, swim, and mingle with the people. In the evenings we went to one of the clubs to listen to the fantastic music and dance until the early hours of the morning.

"Our favorite street in Havana was the Paseo del Prado. It was a beautiful street lined with trees and marble benches. It started at the beach, passed lovely palatial homes, and led to the shopping and entertainment district. Walter P. decided to recreate that street, on a very small scale, in the Jungle. He determined people along Boca Ciega Bay needed to have their own shopping and entertainment area. Why should they have to go downtown for everything? Why couldn't entertainment and shopping be located right in their neighborhood? Walter P. felt sure people would love it.

"He decided he would name the area Jungle Prado, after the Havana Boulevard. Walter P. started looking at his property to find the perfect location for the new shopping mecca. He had several requirements for the site. It had to be where people could get to it easily by both land and water. It needed to be scenic enough that people would enjoy coming for the view as well as the amenities. There should be impressive homes nearby so that it felt like you were in an exclusive area. And there was one final requirement for the location—it had to be on land that had no market value.

The Indian Shell Mound, St. Petersburg, Fla.

One of the many shell mounds around St. Petersburg in the early 1900's
Photo from the State Archives of Florida

"The site of the old Indian village and burial grounds at the end of Elbow Lane was the only piece of his land that fit all those requirements. Today he would not be allowed to build there, but in 1923 nothing prevented him from using the land. There were no laws about building over native burial grounds. In fact, people all around the Pinellas Peninsula regularly dug up and built over Indian sites. There were no Tocobaga left to protest."

I remembered the stories that Clara had told me the other day about the Tocobaga. It made me sad to think that the people who lived here for so many years had essentially been forgotten. I wondered how much history had been lost when people indiscriminately cleared the land, not caring about those who had once thought of this area as their home.

Clara continued, "That section of land had been avoided by people for years, because almost everyone believed it was haunted. Walter P. felt he would never be able to sell it. Seeing the land sitting there, unused and totally unprofitable, had bothered him for a long time. Now he had a use for it, and his instinct told him it would be a money maker.

"There had been a pier at the site, but it had been destroyed by the hurricane. People had asked for it to be rebuilt, but Walter P. saw no financial benefit in doing that. However, if he built his Jungle Prado there, then rebuilding the old pier would make financial sense. He could make everyone happy.

"I was horrified when Thomas told me about Walter P.'s plans. I knew the spirits would not be happy to have their resting place destroyed. I tried to explain that this had been a sacred spot for the Tocobaga; Walter P. didn't care. He brought in men, shovels, and machines. I watched in dismay as they began to flatten the mounds. Remains were scattered everywhere. The spirits did not like having their resting place destroyed, but what the spirits thought did not bother Walter P. at all.

"I have always wondered if the spirits got their revenge by putting a curse on the building. Walter P. never had the success with the shopping complex that he had hoped he would have. Even today no restaurant at the location seems to be able to last for more than a few years. Workers, in whatever restaurant happens to be there at the time, talk about strange sightings and odd happenings. Some say there are parts of the building where they will not go alone or after dark."

While I found all this very interesting, so far I had not heard anything about a tiger or the Gangplank. The tea table appeared and Clara suggested we take a break. I decided that as soon as tea was finished I would remind her about what I wanted to know.

When we finished Clara said, "The Gangplank!! Those times are some of my favorite memories." I breathed a sigh of relief. Clara gave me a reproachful look, "I really am getting to what you want to hear.

"We were excited about the opening of the Jungle Prado in 1924. It had everything: a full service gas station and garage, a flower market, a grocery, a women's apparel shop, a store that sold decorative items for the home, a drug store with a soda fountain, and a nightclub. But just like the restaurants today, none of the businesses ever seemed to last for long.

"The most successful part of the venue was the Gangplank nightclub, the first speakeasy in St. Petersburg. It caught on quickly. Walter P. once told us it grossed six thousand dollars a week. That would be about eighty thousand dollars today!

It became the place to go, and stayed that way for several years. All drinks were required to be served in teacups, and no matter what might be in the cup you always referred to it as tea. Prohibition had been in effect for over four years. Having a place where we could meet friends, have a cup of tea, and enjoy great entertainment was exactly what we needed. Every night the Gangplank was filled.

"I am not sure why Walter P. decided to include a speakeasy in the complex. He hadn't been a drinker. If his father had still been here I doubt it would have happened, but when Walter moved to North Carolina Walter P. took things in a different direction. He probably thought he could make money from it, and he did.

"The speakeasy must have been in the plans from the very beginning because the complex was built over a well-designed tunnel that led down to the water. Walter P. swore the tunnel's inclusion was for the sole purpose of making it easy to bring up the food and supplies that arrived by boat. I am sure the passage was used for that, but it also made it easy to bring in bootlegged liquor without being seen. The tunnel's design, with lots of secreted storage spaces, also made it very easy to hide things.

"Walter P. knew that other speakeasies would soon begin opening around town. If the Gangplank was to keep its spot as the place to go, there would have to be something more than plentiful liquor. In Havana we had places where we always went because we knew there would be good food, great music and entertainment. Walter P. decided that would be the standard for the Gangplank. He didn't have a hard time getting entertainers to come to Florida during season, and he got the best. I enjoyed all of them, but Count Basie and Duke Ellington were, without a doubt, my favorites.

"Thomas was doing quite a bit of work for Walter P., and one of the benefits was that we could always get a table at the Gangplank anytime we came. Most evenings we stopped by to have a drink, listen to the music, and dance. The patio at the west end of the Gangplank had been designed to look like the prow of a boat, and on nice evenings the bands played out there. We listened to the music by the water and danced under the stars."

Clara smiled and said, "Probably at least half of the stories you hear about the Gangplank are not true. It is amazing how many things people think they remember happening that didn't. This story, however, I know is true because I was there when it happened.

"One of the entertainers at the Gangplank was a dancer named Paige, P-A-I-G-E; only she pronounced it 'Pay-gee.' Being a talented dancer, and very attractive, she had a large following among the gentlemen. Paige always wore a short tiger dress which fastened with a small strap over one shoulder.

"I had come to the Gangplank to meet Thomas. He and Walter P. still had some work to finish, so they suggested I go in and watch the rehearsal for the evening show. The Gangplank's shows were fairly elaborate productions. Paige happened to be the lead dancer in the number they were practicing, and she had on her usual tiger dress. About halfway through the dance the strap broke on her outfit and it fell straight to the floor! I won't say she was totally nude under the costume, but the little she had on left nothing to the imagination. She never blinked or missed a step, though most of the band members and other dancers did. She finished the number, picked up her costume, and walked off the stage.

"I sat in shock! I had heard of things like this happening in other cities, but not in St. Petersburg! I turned around. There, standing right behind me, were Walter P. and Thomas. Both of their mouths were hanging open and their eyes were bulging! We all looked at each other and burst into laughter. Walter P. said he bet they would have a big crowd that evening, and he was right. In fact, for the next couple of weeks the crowds were huge. No one moved during Paige's performance, even the waiters stopped in anticipation. Paige, however, made sure the costume was well mended and it never fell off again, much to the disappointment of many of her fans."

I listened to Clara with fascination. Her life had been much more interesting than mine. She had met so many people and had such great experiences. I was a little envious of her.

"Don't be," Clara said softly, once again reading my thoughts. "Remember, my life has finished, but yours hasn't. Enjoy what you have, make your own memories, and don't wish for something that isn't here. I can see you are very anxious to go over to the Gangplank. Go ahead; we can talk more when we see each other again."

I walked up to Elbow Lane. The first thing I noticed was that Clara seemed to be prophetic. The restaurant that had been there just a few days before had a "Closed" sign across the front. A placard on the lawn said a new restaurant would be opening soon. This end of the building had been well kept by the owners of the various establishments located there. At some point the front section of the building had been enlarged. One of the previous owners had proudly pointed out to me that the original façade, with its beautiful arches, was now located in the middle of the dining room.

Walking to the west end of the building, I saw the outside entertainment area Clara had told me about. It did look like the prow of a boat. I sat down on the wall around the neglected patio and thought about how things had changed since the building's heyday.

The Gangplank had been at the end of the building closest to the water. It has been divided and is now the location of businesses and apartments. Looking at the complex from where I sat I would have never guessed that it had been one of the most popular places in St. Petersburg at one time. The section behind the restaurant has been neglected and needs care. What were once little shops are now apartments, all appearing rundown and tired looking. A large beautiful condo has been built right behind the building and partially blocks the view of the Bay.

Another change to the complex happened many years ago when someone altered the name from Jungle Prado to Jungle Prada. If you call the building by its original name you will be quickly corrected. Few people today know about the alteration, they think it has always been that way.

There is still a pier, and it has been newly redone. I watched someone launching a boat and saw people fishing off the dock. The pier has benches where you can sit and enjoy wonderful view of the Bay. Across the parking lot is what remains of the Indian Sacred Grounds. They are now protected and cannot be leveled for another building.

As I sat there I could imagine people dancing under the stars with the moonlight shining on the water and soft breezes blowing through the trees. For some reason I began to feel a little sad, and after a few minutes I rose to start back home.

I had only gone a few steps when I heard music. I stopped to listen. It was Duke Ellington singing, "It Don't Mean a Thing If It Ain't Got That Swing!" It seemed to be coming from the patio I had just left. I turned around and the music stopped. The patio sat empty except for a few leaves blowing in the wind. I waited quietly but heard only silence.

Probably someone in one of the apartments had turned on a radio. I started walking and heard the music again. The tones were rich and clear. It was not coming from anyone's apartment. I knew it would stop if I turned around, so I stood quietly for a few minutes listening. I found myself swaying in time to the music. I think I would have stayed there all afternoon, but I saw people coming across the parking lot and they were looking at me with concern.

I slowly started walking again. The music grew softer and by the time I reached the street it had faded away. I was wishing I could have held on to the music when I heard Clara say, "Make your own memories!"

To me, 'drink responsibly' means don't spill it.

ANONYMOUS

THE SOUTH SIDE FIZZ

8-10 mint leaves	1½ Tbs. simple syrup
2oz. gin	¾ oz. lemon juice
Ice	club soda

Muddle mint leaves in a shaker. Add gin, lemon juice, and simple sugar. Stir to dissolve. Fill shaker with large pieces of ice and shake gently. Strain into a highball glass filled with ice cubes and top with club soda.

The story is that this was the preferred beverage of Al Capone and his crew. The South Side Fizz's name is linked to Chicago's south side, which Al Capone and his gang ran. The north side booze runners were bringing in a smoother gin to their speakeasies—which only needed a splash of ginger ale to be divine. But the south side gin had a much rougher bite, so more elements were demanded to make it drinkable.

Walter P. Fuller and Eve Alsman's wedding, 1923

Photo from St. Petersburg Museum of History

It is impossible to live without failing at something, unless you live so cautiously that you might as well not lived at all, in which case you have failed by default.

J. K. ROWLING

The Jungle Hotel

A frail, elderly woman stood on the sidewalk partially blocking my path. She looked lost, so I stopped and asked if I could help. She stared at me for a moment as though she was trying to decide whether she could trust me or not.

Then she sighed, "I am so confused! This looks like the right place but the name is wrong. It says Admiral Farragut Academy, and I'm looking for the Jungle Hotel."

She seemed to be close to tears. I told her that she was at the right place. At one time this had been the Jungle Hotel, but the Academy had bought the building many years ago.

A look of relief passed over her face and she seemed to relax. I waited for a moment or two to make sure she would be okay and then turned to continue my walk. That was when I heard her say, rather regally, "You know my husband built this hotel."

That got my attention! I knew there was only one way that what she had just said could be true. I looked at her closely trying to see if she was in another dimension, but I couldn't tell. The petite, white haired woman certainly looked old enough to have been Walter P.'s wife.

The woman saw a low wall and asked if I would mind sitting with her for a bit. My curiosity had been aroused so I agreed and we sat down. For a few minutes she didn't say anything. She seemed to know I was aware that Walter P. had built the former hotel. When she finally began to speak, she spoke so softly I could hardly hear her.

"I met my husband when we were both working as reporters for the St. Petersburg Times. I fell in love with him almost immediately. We had common aims for life and we enjoyed each other's company. To me it was obvious he was destined for bigger things and that we belonged together."

Her voice seemed to be getting stronger. I looked at her and realized that she wasn't nearly as old as I had first thought.

Smiling, she continued, "We were married on June 15, 1923. It was a time to be adventuresome and take chances. Walter P. had spent his whole life following in his father's footsteps. He sold the land his father had purchased and developed the areas his father had planned, but the time had come for him to make his own path. I helped him see new directions.

"Prohibition had been in effect for three years and speakeasies were the rage all over the country, but there wasn't one in St. Petersburg. I believed we should open a speakeasy. Walter P. didn't drink at that time and resisted the idea until he learned how profitable they could be. When we opened the Gangplank it immediately became the hottest place in town.

"One evening I overheard a man complaining about having trouble finding a place to stay. He said he didn't know why we hadn't opened a hotel around the nightclub. I knew that had to be our next endeavor and it didn't take much to sell Walter P. on the idea.

"There were a lot of hotels and boarding houses in St. Petersburg, but none of them really fit the modern tourist. The Sunset Hotel, just down the street, was perfect for the people who stayed there. Their guests were mostly older and well-to-do. They arrived by train, with more baggage than you could imagine, and stayed for the whole season. They came back to the same place every year because they knew everyone. They liked the pleasant family atmosphere, the genteel entertainment, and the quiet evenings."

I thought the woman had probably given a fairly accurate description of the people who stayed at the Sunset. Clara and Marie had both mentioned that the residents were older and how much fun they had at Tent City. However, I knew Clara would never have stayed there for all those years if it had been as boring as the woman made it sound.

"Thank goodness things were changing!" she continued. "It was the age of the automobile, not the train. Modern tourists were looking for something totally different from what their parents and grandparents wanted. They had no intention of bring everything they owned with them when they traveled. They expected a hotel with large luxuriously furnished rooms and lots of activities. Their goal wasn't to feel like they were home, their aim was to see new things and have different experiences."

She paused for a bit and looked around. "The right location was critical for the hotel's success. It had to have space for lots of activities. The site had to be beautiful and seem exotic, but it couldn't feel isolated. It needed to be easy to get to, and it had to be near the water.

"Only one place around the Gangplank met all those requirements, and that was the location of the Jungle Country Club. It had everything we needed: a golf course, tennis courts, plenty of room for riding paths, a boat basin across the street, beautiful views, and lots of open space. The Gangplank was just a few blocks away, people could get into town easily on the trolley, and it would be close to the new airfield Walter P. had planned.

"Walter P. had some reservations, but he finally agreed to the location. We began working on the design of the hotel. I imagined it as luxurious and exotic while my husband had in mind golf and fun. We realized that it needed to be a combination of both of our ideas. We wanted our guests to feel like they had come to a magnificent, tropical getaway where they were going to have a good time.

"We decided on a three hundred room Mediterranean-style hotel. Walter P. insisted that construction needed to be started as soon as possible. He got a loan but it wasn't enough for what we had planned. I felt we should delay construction until we could get all of the money we needed. However, my husband knew there were several hotels being planned and he felt it was imperative to get ours open as soon as possible.

"To make the loan work, Walter P. cut the number of the rooms down to one hundred and suggested I make alterations in the décor of the hotel. I would not compromise! The furnishings were expensive but they were what our guests would expect. I reminded him that we were saving money by only furnishing one hundred rooms, and I refused to change anything I had planned. Walter P. wasn't happy but he agreed to let me continue."

I took another look at the woman sitting next to me. Either she was getting younger as she sat there or my eyes were playing strange tricks on me! I couldn't imagine how I had ever seen her as old. I doubted she was even forty.

Her voice sounded strong and excited as she continued, "The hotel was perfect! Guests knew as they came up the beautiful curved drive, and saw the banners and flags hanging across the front of the building, that they had arrived at a special place. Flamingos covered the ceiling in the lobby, and palm trees and fountains filled the patio. The elegant dining room seated two hundred and fifty people and had a mural of a band of pirates at one end.

"The Hotel had all the latest conveniences, but I designed it to give the impression it had been here for years. The furnishings were from Spain and had been brought in on barges. Almost every piece was an antique.

"Our guests demanded entertainment, but not things like teas, friendly card games, lectures, or croquet. They wanted to go deep sea fishing and horseback riding. They expected to be able to play golf and tennis as well as swim and go boating. They wanted readily-available liquor and lively music. We did our best to make sure our guests' wishes were met. Besides the golf course we had a riding stable and tennis courts. We offered sailing lessons, hired dancing instructors to teach the latest dance steps, provided excursions to the hottest gambling spots, and for the real adventurers we offered flying lessons.

"We had excellent chefs, but the people who stayed with us expected dining to be more than good food. They wanted an experience with a live band and dancing. After dinner our lodgers had no intention of retiring to their rooms for a quiet evening; as far as they were concerned the night was just beginning. They had come to have fun!"

I was fascinated hearing her talk about the hotel. I could picture the elegantly dressed couples swirling around the dance floor. However, I knew those good times hadn't lasted. During the early part of World War II the Jungle Hotel had been a training facility for the Army Air Corps, and I knew that the Academy had bought the building before the end of the War. I wondered what happened.

A 1930 view of the Jungle Hotel

Photo from St. Petersburg Museum of History

Teeing off on the Jungle Golf Course outside the Hotel, 1927

Photo Courtesy Tampa-Hillsborough County Public Library System

When Mrs. Fuller spoke again, I heard a change of tone in her voice. "The hotel only stayed open during season, and we always had to turn people away. Things were going so well that we started talking about enlarging the Jungle. I couldn't see how anything could stop us from doing bigger and better things. We were fully booked and making final preparations for the 1930 season when everything fell apart. On October 29, 1929, the stock market crashed. We felt the effects immediately. Within a few days almost every reservation had been cancelled.

"Walter P. tried to assure me that this was just a temporary setback. He believed that in a year or two things would be back to normal. He had faced hard times before and had always come out okay. This time that didn't happen. He lost the hotel and almost everything else he owned. He held on to the Gangplank for a couple years but then that, too, was gone. Our marriage wasn't strong enough to survive everything happening around us and it also ended."

She stared sadly for a few moments and then turned to me and asked if I had ever stayed at the hotel. When I shook my head no she wanted to know why. She had to be joking! I told her it would have been impossible for that to have happened.

She looked me, and I saw her note my well-worn shorts, old shirt, and walking shoes. Rather condescendingly she said, "Well, I guess I'm really not surprised. It did cost between ten dollars and fifteen dollars a day to stay there, and even though that included meals, ordinary people could not afford it. My husband always said it was the swankiest place in town."

Her attitude irritated me. I reached in the pocket of my shorts and pulled out the twenty dollar bill I had grabbed before I left home. I asked if that would cover a night's stay. Luckily, she didn't seem to know anything about inflation. Her eyes grew big, and being much more respectful she asked, "If you had the money, why didn't you ever stay there?"

Why did she keep asking me about staying at the hotel? I'm sure she could hear the frustration in my voice when I told her I couldn't have stayed there.

The hotel had been sold to the Academy over seventy years ago. I hadn't even been born at that time!

She looked at me in shock. "You hadn't been born! That can't be true! You can see me and you have been talking to me. What is going on?"

Finally I understood. She thought I was in her dimension! I didn't know what to say or how to explain it. Sighing, I told her I didn't know why or how it was possible, it just was.

A party without cake is just a meeting.

Julia Child

RITZ CARLTON 1920's LEMON POUND CAKE

3 cups all-purpose flour	1 Tbs. baking powder
¾ tsp. salt	3 cups of sugar
1 cup unsalted butter at room temperature	
½ cup shortening	5 large eggs
1 cup whole milk	6 Tbs. lemon Juice
Zest of one lemon	

Preheat oven to 350°.

Spray and flour one large Bundt pan or two 9x5 loaf pans.

Cream butter, shortening and sugar. Add eggs one at a time, beating until well blended.

Add dry ingredients in three additions, alternating with milk. Begin and end with flour mixture. Beat at low speed until just blended after each addition. Mix in lemon juice and zest.

Pour batter into prepared pans. Bake about 55 minutes or until tester inserted into the center comes out clean. Cool cake in the pan for 15 minutes. Turn cake out onto rack and cool.

Icing: 2 cups of powdered sugar and ¼ cup of lemon juice mixed well. Poke holes in cake with a toothpick and pour icing over cake.

The Sunset Hotel in 1920

Photo from the St. Petersburg Museum of History

Do not educate your children to be rich, educate them to be happy.
So when they grow up they will know the value of things, not
the price.

ANONYMOUS

Hard Times

As Mrs. Fuller and I sat there, I saw Clara walking up the street. When she reached us she gave the woman next to me a hug and said it was good to see her again. Clara asked if we had had a pleasant afternoon. I told her it had been very interesting, and that I had been learning about the Jungle Hotel from Mrs. Fuller. The woman's eyes widened when she realized that Clara and I could also see each other, but she didn't say anything.

Clara said we obviously had not been introduced, because this was not Mrs. Fuller. I looked at her in shock; the woman had told me that she and Walter P. were married! Clara then introduced me to Eve Alsman, adding that she was Walter P.'s second wife.

It had never even been mentioned that Walter P. had a wife. If Eve was his "second" wife, how many wives had he had? Evidently both women knew what I was thinking. Eve looked amused and Clara smiled and said, "Just three dear, just three."

Eve turned to me and said she had enjoyed the afternoon. She added that she hoped we could talk again sometime. I thanked her for sharing her memories, and then she disappeared.

Clara looked thoughtful, "Walter P. made some big changes after he met Eve. He went from being a teetotaler to becoming a steady drinker. He stopped socializing with many of the friends he had known over the years and got involved with a new group of people.

"Eve and I were never close companions, but she was Walter P.'s wife and we did do things together. After she and Walter P. divorced she dropped out of our circle. I was astonished to find out she had returned. She has been gone for so long. One thing I will have to say about her though, she did a wonderful job on the Jungle Hotel. I hope she told you all about it. No one knew that hotel better than she did, not even Walter P."

Clara and I started walking back down the street. "I think Eve always thought we were upset about the Jungle Hotel being built so close to the Sunset, but no one was. We all knew it was just a matter of time before another hotel came into the area, and we were glad Walter P. was the one building it. We knew the Jungle would not be a threat to the Sunset. They were two different types of hotels for two different types of people. We looked forward to the new hotel and the people and excitement it would bring to the area.

"The Jungle Hotel opened on February 10, 1926. While season was almost over, Walter P. made a wise decision in opening when he did. People had a chance to see the Jungle in all its beauty and luxury. Before season ended the hotel was almost fully booked for the following year. Several new hotels opened in St. Petersburg the next year, but the Jungle had been established in many people's minds as the place to stay.

"The hotel's opening was a gala affair. Eve and Walter P. referred to it as the 'social event of the season.' I would call that a bit of an exaggeration, but everyone did have a wonderful time. The Fullers invited two hundred and fifty people from all across the country to be their guests for the evening. Thomas and I received an invitation.

"As guests arrived they were escorted into the dining room and presented to the Fullers. Eve was a gracious hostess and she looked lovely. She wore a pale green gown and had a huge bouquet of orchids on her shoulder. Walter P., in his tuxedo and white tie, proudly greeted everyone as an old friend.

"Each guest received a little treasure chest as a favor. The ladies' chests held a lovely handkerchief, while those for the men contained golf tees and trinkets. Dinner was a lavish six course affair. The new chefs prepared a splendid meal, and between every course there was entertainment.

"After dinner we were ushered into one of the lounges where Walter P. and Eve had a special evening planned for us. To everyone's surprise and delight Walter P. presented the McGees! They had danced in several movies, which we'd all seen. Their numbers were fantastic and they had beautiful costumes. I would have loved to have been able to move that gracefully. After the McGees, the evening took a more cultural turn as we enjoyed a wonderful ballet. The night ended with our dancing to the music of the hotel orchestra, the Jungle Serenaders. It was a delightful evening.

"The opening of the hotel meant extra work for many of Walter P.'s employees, especially the musicians. They played at the hotel during dinner and then went to the Gangplank for the rest of the evening. Walter P. paid his people well, but he expected to get his money's worth from them. There was a radio station at the hotel which broadcast live music for two hours each evening. You could listen to the orchestra in your own home as they played for hotel guests during dinner and for dancing afterwards.

"While the Jungle was being built, Walter P. told us he needed an airport. He said people were starting to fly down and he wanted them to be able to land close to the hotel. He built the Piper-Fuller Flying Field, which was where Tyrone Square Mall is now. It had two 300 foot runways and twin-winged planes regularly used it.

"Needing a place for his guests to land sounded good, but I believe the main reason Walter P. built the field was so that he could fly in liquor. Everyone knew he was bootlegging, but bringing in enough alcohol for the Gangplank and the Jungle had gotten almost impossible. Boats coming through the Bay were regularly stopped and searched. Any illegal cargo was confiscated.

"We heard that early every morning a plane would land at the field and taxi into the hanger. The plane was quickly unloaded and the cargo would be immediately taken from the premises. None of us knew what was on those planes, but we had our suspicions. Walter P. had moved his office into the hangar when he built the air field, and the pilots of those early morning flights always left a quart of whisky outside the door of his office. He liked to joke that each morning he found a gift left by the booze fairy."

Clara and I walked quietly for a while. I thought about all I had learned that afternoon. Eve said they had lost the Jungle Hotel when the stock market crashed in 1929. I asked Clara what happened.

"That was a rough time for everyone. Walter P. believed that, like all the other times, things would quickly return to normal. His uncle took over ownership of the hotel, but Walter P. felt sure that within a year or two he would be able to repurchase the hotel.

"The Depression turned out to be much worse than Walter P. expected. Few people had money to travel, and staying in a hotel was a luxury that most could not afford. Hotels and businesses everywhere closed. The Fullers did everything they could to hold on to the Jungle Hotel. They even sold the beautiful furniture and artwork, but there were no guests. Eventually the building had to be sold."

Clara hadn't mentioned anything about the Sunset, so I asked what happened to it when the market crashed.

"That year was a disaster for every hotel, including the Sunset. The next year the Sunset was leased to a man who had managed several hotels, including the Belleview Biltmore in Clearwater and the Flamingo in Miami Beach. While he had his choice of any hotel in this area, including the Jungle and the Rolyat, he chose the Sunset. That was probably what saved it. In 1930, the Sunset opened in mid-December as usual. It wasn't full, but it didn't feel empty either. Several of us were able to come back, and the manager persuaded some of his past clients to stay at the hotel."

Clara and I had walked back to Sunset Park. Work had begun at the hotel and people were there almost every day. Clara said things seemed to be mostly in a cleanup and planning stage, but a caretaker/guard had moved into the building. That meant we could no longer sit on the porch, drink tea, and visit. Fortunately the days were getting longer and warmer, so we had begun spending our time walking or sitting in the park.

Jokingly, I had told Clara I didn't mind not being able to sit on the porch, but I did miss the tea. When we arrived at the park I saw a little table by the bench where we usually sat. On the table was a tea set from the hotel. Clara smiled when she saw it, "I told the staff how much you liked their tea. They volunteered to set it up over here anytime we wanted it. Things can be noisy in the hotel so it is really much nicer here anyway."

I had loved this tea from the moment I had taken my first sip. Gratefully, I picked up my cup and took a drink. I asked Clara how she felt about the renovation to the hotel.

She thought for a bit, "I am not sure how I feel about it. I will have to see what they are going to do, but at least they are fixing it up and not tearing it down. It has been in such a state of disrepair for so long." She looked over at the hotel lovingly, "The Sunset started out as a luxury hotel, but as they built bigger and fancier places to stay it began to lose some of its luster. The funny thing is, out of all the hotels along this side of the Bay, the Sunset is the only one that is still here." Smiling, she said, "I'm so glad, because as long as it is here my friends and I can return."

The man who has nothing to boast of but his ancestors is like a potato—the only good part of him is under ground.

SIR THOMAS OVERBURY

Frieda Hemple's Potato Salad

Use small potatoes and boil in skin. Take out of water as hot as possible and remove skin. Then cut into thin slices and place in bowl. Pour much good olive oil on potatoes and sprinkle with salt. Allow to draw for ten minutes. After ten minutes, pour on the potatoes a cupful of meat-bouillon or meat-extract. Season to taste with pepper, onions, and mustard dissolved in vinegar. Do not stir with spoon, but shake the bowl vigorously. Let stand for ten minutes and it is then ready to serve.

It is important that the bowl should be kept covered whenever possible, and that it should be kept standing in hot water so that when served it will be warm. Another important thing is to use plenty of oil to keep the salad well moistened.

Good Housekeeping-1916 "All-Star Recipes" pg. 84

Rolyat Hotel shortly after opening in 1927

Photo from the St. Petersburg Museum of History

Sometimes it's not the people who change; it's the mask that falls off.

ANONYMOUS

Handsome Jack Taylor

Sitting in Sunset Park with fog swirling around me, I waited for Clara. The sea fog is always bad in February and March, because the air temperatures are warm but the Gulf waters are still cool. The fog seemed to mute the sounds, and I smiled as I thought about how Clara complains about the street noises and traffic. She's still upset about the causeway across Boca Ciega Bay that they built in 1939. If she could have her way Central Avenue would still end at Park Street.

I thought I saw Clara walking toward me, but to my surprise I realized it was Eve. The young woman smiled, "I'm glad to see you again! I've been asking about you and I hear you're interested in the history of the area." She paused a moment, "Have you ever been to the Rolyat Hotel?"

Her question puzzled me. What was it with this woman and hotels where I might have stayed?

Eve shook her head, "I know you couldn't have stayed there, but I wondered if you had ever been there."

I told her I didn't think so. I said I had never even heard the name until Clara recently mentioned it. Eve wanted to know how the Rolyat had come into our conversation. I explained that Clara had mentioned it when we were talking about the Depression and how it affected the hotels around here.

Eve looked relieved, "That's Jake. I wanted to tell you about it but I was afraid she might have already done it."

"Wait a minute!" I interrupted. "Who's Jake? I've never heard of him."

Eve actually laughed at me! "If I had any question about you not being one of us, you just answered it. Jake isn't a person, it means 'alright.' If you say something is 'Jake' you mean it's okay.

"You do know the Rolyat; you just know it by a different name. It's the Stetson University Law School." She paused, and I'm sure I heard a note of glee in her voice when she said, "Handsome Jack would be so upset if he found out people have already forgotten about him and his hotel! It serves him right. He was a real four-flusher!"

I had a feeling this might be a very confusing conversation. Who was Handsome Jack and what was a four-flusher?

Eve nodded, "I'm not surprised you don't know four-flusher. It means to pretend to have money that you don't. As for Jack, you're gonna like hearing about him.

"I introduced Jack Taylor to Walter P., but I'm sure they would have eventually met on their own. Jack was charming and flamboyant. He was also arrogant, self-centered and a total con man. He said people usually called him 'Handsome Jack.' I'm sure he gave himself that name.

"He claimed to have been born in New Hampshire and bragged about his ancestry and his family's accomplishments. He seemed to know everyone of importance on the East Coast and regularly dropped names of the rich and famous. The problem, as we later learned, was that none of it was true. The people Jack regularly talked about swore they had never met him. He didn't come from a long line of rich, accomplished, East Coast residents; his parents were immigrants from Eastern Europe. His name wasn't really Jack Taylor, and I didn't think he was handsome.

"He told everyone he had been a successful banker in Boston and New York, and that he had lived and worked in Europe. The statements were true as far as they went, but he forgot a few important details. The money he made as a banker came from fake stock promotions, and when the scams were discovered he had to move to Europe to keep from being arrested.

"When he returned from the continent he was introduced to Evelyn DuPont, heiress to the DuPont fortune. Jack told everyone when they met it was love at first sight. We were sure the 'they' he meant was he and Evelyn's money, not he and Evelyn. Jack believed once they married he would have the DuPont fortune to spend as he pleased.

"Unfortunately for him, when the DuPonts saw his interest in their daughter they did some research into his background. They were shocked by what they learned. The family tried to talk Evelyn out of marrying him, but she refused to listen. Finally, in desperation, they told her if she married Jack they would cut her off from the family fortune. She and Jack didn't believe that would, or could, happen. They were wrong. The moment the marriage became official Evelyn was disinherited. Jack's access to the DuPont money was gone forever!

"Jack and Evelyn were newlyweds when they arrived in St. Petersburg the day after the 1921 hurricane. He claimed to be surprised at the weather and told us they had made plans to come to St. Petersburg for their honeymoon months ago. He said they had been so busy with the wedding plans that they hadn't heard about the hurricane. People had doubts about that when Jack immediately started buying up beachfront property at greatly reduced prices. Most of us came to believe that he came down here because he had heard about the hurricane.

"Jack and Evelyn were 'puttin' on the Ritz' from the moment they arrived. Evelyn seemed to have closets full of expensive clothes and she always looked glamorous! Her hair was set in the latest styles and she wore exquisite jewelry. They were chauffeured around town in matching Daimler touring cars. We thought they were real eggs.

"Jack talked about the DuPonts and other East Coast swells in every conversation. He told us how they were giving him advice and financing his decisions, so people listened closely to what he had to say."

Eggs! Swells! Ritz! What in the world was Eve talking about? When Clara said someone looked swell it meant they looked nice. So, were East Coast swells people on the East Coast who dressed nicely? Ritz was a cracker or a hotel, but how could you put on either one of those? And what in the world did she mean by an egg? I didn't have a clue if it was good or bad.

Eve apologized, "I'm sorry. 'Swell' can mean nice or it can mean a very rich man. It just depends on how it is used. An 'egg' is someone who is absurdly wealthy and lives extravagantly. 'Puttin' on the Ritz' means to dress fashionably."

Eve continued with her story. "Evelyn and I quickly became friends. She was a bit of a Dumb Dora, a little naive, and totally spoiled. But she could be charming, well-mannered, and fun to be with. She and Jack loved the

Gangplank and they always sat at our table when they came. I liked Jack in the beginning. We all did. None of us had ever met anyone who knew so many famous people and had such wonderful stories. We believed everything he told us.

"Jack and Walter P. became good friends. Later, I realized that Walter P.'s total acceptance of what Jack said was surprising. Walter P. could be a bit of a con artist himself, so it seemed strange that he never questioned or doubted any of Jack's stories. Even after Jack left St. Petersburg in disgrace, Walter P. still believed that Jack had just had a run of bad luck.

"My husband encouraged Jack to get into land sales and suggested the Davista area would be a good place for him to start. Walter P. owned the land in that area, but he had never gotten around to developing it. If he could sell some of those sections to Jack then Walter P. could put all his focus on the Jungle, which was what he wanted to do.

"They reached an agreement on the sale of the land, and Jack and Evelyn arrived at the attorney's office one evening to complete the deal. The land was valued at half a million dollars, so five thousand dollars had to be put down to close the deal. Jack announced to the group that Evelyn had the money. She turned her back, lifted the skirt on her gown, rolled down her stocking, and peeled a ten thousand dollar bill off her leg.

"Walter P. claimed he was so shocked he couldn't move, but evidently he recovered quickly. He looked at her leg close enough he could tell there were six more bills of the same denomination on it.

"Everyone was impressed, as they were supposed to be. No one knew, other than Jack and Evelyn, that those seven bills were all the money they had in this world. Technically it wasn't even their money; it was the end of the money from Jack's stock market scam.

"There ended up being a problem with closing the deal that evening. No one had change for a ten thousand dollar bill. The banks were closed until the next morning, and Jack refused to take a check from any of the men. He said he had found you couldn't trust people.

"The following morning, when the bank opened and change could be made, the sale was completed. Jack and Evelyn walked out of the bank proudly. They had convinced some of the most important men in town they had so much money that they typically walked around carrying tens of thousands of dollars.

"The first thing Jack did after buying the land was to change the name. He was planning an upscale community, and Davista did not sound exclusive enough to him. He renamed the area Pasadena-on-the-Gulf. Walter gave him permission to use the plans they had for developing the area, and Jack got things going immediately. He laid out the subdivisions, had a water system installed, and gas lines put in. Then Jack did something no one else around here had ever done—he built a home in each section to showcase what that area would look like when houses were finished. It was a swell idea."

Eve paused for a moment. When she went on with her story I could hear a slightly different tone to her voice. "Even though Jack and Walter P. were friends, Jack envied Walter P.'s standing and financial success. When we announced plans for the Jungle Hotel in 1925, Jack quickly stated he would be building a luxury hotel in the Pasadena area. It would be called the Rolyat, which was Taylor spelled backwards. His plans included a golf course which would be designed by Walter Hagen, one of the top golfers in the country. Walter had won the U.S. Open twice, and he was the first American to win the British Open. Jack said his course would be for the best players. He was sure regular golfers would want to continue to play at the Jungle.

"I was livid, but Walter P. took it all in stride. He said there were more than enough people coming down here to fill two hotels and two golf courses. He didn't care if Jack built a hotel, too.

"Jack began, secretly, to make plans to upstage us by having the Rolyat in business before we could open the Jungle. He assigned Evelyn to find out how and when we planned to launch our hotel. At first I was flattered by her questions, but I began to wonder why she was so curious. I finally asked. Not being the sharpest knife in the drawer, Evelyn whispered that Jack planned to have the Rolyat open before we had the inauguration for the Jungle. I couldn't believe it!

"I told Walter P. and he said not to worry about it. The Rolyat was several weeks behind us in construction, so that couldn't happen. My husband turned out to be wrong! Even though the hotel was only partially finished, Jack opened the Rolyat three weeks ahead of us. As usual, he went overboard. He had the fountain in front of the hotel filled with champagne, and his guests of honor were Babe Ruth, Walter Hagen, and an opera diva from New York by the name of Frieda Hempel."

Just then we heard a sound behind us, Eve and I both turned to see Clara standing there. She walked around the bench, sat next to Eve, and asked gently if she could tell the next part of the story.

Eve nodded and Clara began, "I think you described it best when you once said Jack's hotel had flash but yours had class. The Rolyat appeared to be wildly successful and the bar was packed every night. It looked like Jack was hitting on all sixes, but things weren't quite as they seemed.

'Handsome' Jack Taylor

African Island in 1925, home to Jack Taylor's monkeys

Photo Courtesy Tampa-Hillsborough County Public Library System

I looked at Clara. What did 'hitting on all sixes' mean? Eve leaned over and said quietly, "That means it seemed like Jack was doing everything perfectly."

Clara nodded, "His plans for lavish spending didn't stop with the hotel. On Central Avenue he put up an elaborate display of colorful birds, and he built an island on the fourth fairway of his golf course where he put a monkey house with twenty monkeys.

"Everyone thought Jack and Evelyn were the most successful couple in town, but in reality they were deeply in debt! They were doing what we called four-flushing. That meant they had been borrowing money from everyone for their extravagant life style. Nothing they had was paid for. A few weeks after opening the hotel, Jack and Evelyn suddenly left town in the middle of the night and never returned.

"I don't think anyone was as surprised as Walter P. when they left. Like Eve told you, he had believed everything Jack said. He considered Jack to be one of his closest friends. Walter P. refused to accept that his pal intentionally ran up debts which he had no plans to pay back.

"Jack and Evelyn made no provisions for anything before they left, including the exotic birds and monkeys. For some reason Walter P. felt responsible for the animals. The birds were beautiful, and he easily found people who would take them. However, the monkeys were a different matter. No one wanted the monkeys!"

Eve laughed, "For some reason, Walter P. took the monkeys over to the Jungle and turned them loose. I don't know if it was the lights, the people, or the music, but the monkeys decided to make the Gangplank their home. They were malicious little things who began tearing the tiles off the roof and throwing them at people. At first everyone thought it was cute, but not for long. When people began hesitating about coming to the Gangplank because of the monkeys, Walter P. knew something had to be done!

"He found a captain preparing to sail out of Tampa who agreed to take the monkeys. They were rounded up, loaded aboard, and the ship sailed off for a foreign port. I always wondered what happened to those monkeys. I doubt that it was a smooth trip for them or anyone else on that ship."

Clara took up the story again, "Evelyn had lost her appeal to Jack once he realized she was really cut off from her family's fortune. They hadn't gotten far into their escape when Jack stopped and filed papers for divorce. He left Evelyn at the courthouse and returned to New York by himself. A friend set him up in a fancy office on Fifth Avenue, and he went back to living the high life.

"Poor Evelyn! She had no money and no idea what to do. She finally got in touch with her family and they rescued her. Eventually, they restored her fortune. We hoped her experience with Jack made her a little wiser, but we doubted it did.

"Jack's leaving caused Walter P. real problems because he had co-signed on the loans for the land. If the loans could not be refinanced Walter P. would lose the land and a lot of money. He stayed optimistic that Jack would get things resolved, but a year later nothing had happened. Walter P. decided to help Jack, so after season he went to New York. There, to his surprise, he found Jack had made no attempt to refinance the loans."

Clara turned to Eve, "While most of us knew things were not going well between the two of you, we couldn't believe Walter P. would run off like that for several months. We felt sorry for you and upset with him."

Clara sighed, "Walter P. learned a lot about Jack on that trip to New York, and none of it was good. He finally had to accept that Jack was not his friend. Walter P. could not get the loans refinanced and lost the land and his money.

"The Rolyat Hotel lasted for three seasons after Jack left, but it could not survive the stock market crash. The golf course stayed open and is still in use today, but the Rolyat closed for good in 1929.

"As far as I know neither Jack nor Evelyn ever returned to this area, and I can't say anyone missed them." Clara looked at Eve and smiled, "Their leaving was Jake with us."

Al Capone

*When I sell liquor, it's called bootlegging. When my patrons
serve it on Lake Shore Drive, it's called hospitality.*

AL CAPONE

Al Capone

The days were getting longer, the weather warmer, and the nights were pleasant. Spring would be here soon. Clara and I had gone for a walk, and we were getting close to the complex that had once held the Gangplank nightclub. The closed restaurant still had a sign in front saying "coming soon." However, since no work appeared to have been started I had my doubts about the "soon" part.

That was why I looked closely at two men dressed in suits and standing in the parking lot. I wondered if they were involved with the new restaurant. The men seemed to be an odd couple. The shorter man made me feel a little uneasy. His eyes never stopped moving and I could tell he didn't miss much around him. He had been watching Clara and me as we walked toward him. The second man had a friendly demeanor and for some reason, even though he was a tall man, the thought that came to my mind was a teddy bear. He also seemed to be paying attention to people walking by, but in his case it seemed more like he hoped to see someone he knew. The men appeared to be friends and laughed and talked easily together.

I asked Clara if she had any idea who the men were. She looked at them, waved, and called out a cheery "Hello!" The teddy bear waved back and said, "Hey Kid!" The other man nodded and simply said, "Clara." Feeling awkward I waved and the men nodded to me. As soon as I thought we would not be overheard I asked Clara who the men were and why they looked so familiar.

She gave me a faint look of amusement. "I am sure you would have eventually figured out who they are, but I doubt you ever met Al Capone and Babe Ruth."

I fought the urge to turn around and stare at the men. Clara had to be kidding. Al Capone had lived in Chicago and Babe Ruth had played for the Yankees. Why would they be at the Gangplank?

Clara nodded, "You're right, people don't usually associate them with this area, but they were friends and they both spent time here. Babe came to St. Petersburg between 1925 and 1935 for spring training. After that he continued to come down to play golf and enjoy the warm winters. Al began coming down when the Yankees started to do their spring training here. He didn't come often or stay long, but he did come.

"The Gangplank was one of their favorite places to go when they were here. I knew Babe, and I liked him. I also met both his wives and his daughters. I didn't know Al well. I never felt comfortable around him, and he wasn't here as much as Babe."

Something struck me as odd about what Clara just said. Why, if she knew Babe Ruth better, had he called her "Kid" while Al Capone had spoken to her by name?

Clara chuckled, "Babe met so many people and he couldn't remember names. He didn't want to offend any of his fans, so he just chose a generic name and used it for everyone. He called most people 'Kid,' but he did give some people another nickname. He would pick out their prominent feature and call them by it. However, it wasn't always flattering. I'd much rather be called 'Kid' than 'Big Ears.'

"Al, on the other hand, found it very important that he could recall exactly who people were. It might well mean the difference between life and death for him."

I had to admit I had not expected to see Babe Ruth and Al Capone when I woke up this morning. My first thought was that nobody was going to believe this. Then, sadly, I realized no one would believe it. More than once I had wanted to talk to someone about one of my adventures with Clara, but I couldn't. Who could I tell? People would wonder about my sanity if I told them I had tea with a ghost at an old, abandoned hotel, or that I saw Al Capone and Babe Ruth chatting in a parking lot.

Clara looked at me. Quietly, she said, "Don't worry, someday you will find a way to share, but for now let's just enjoy our time together."

We walked for a while in silence. I suddenly realized how unusual it was for Clara to be quiet that long and I looked at her. While I couldn't see anyone or hear anybody, somehow I knew she was in a conversation. I waited quietly, not wanting to interrupt.

Finally, she turned to me, "I'm sorry. I wanted to check with Thomas before I told you anything. He remembers this much better than I do."

Thomas! Thomas was here! In my mind he had become more or less a fictional character because he never seemed to be around. Shocked, I didn't pay any attention to where I was walking and caught my toe on an upraised part of the sidewalk. I began to fall and frantically searched for something to grab on to. Suddenly, I felt a hand on my arm, steadying me, pulling me back to my feet. In gratitude I turned to thank whoever had saved me, but no one was there.

Clara looked on anxiously. "Thank you, Thomas!" she said. She paused for a moment and with an amused look on her face she whispered, "Thomas says I am to give you his thanks for keeping me busy and out of trouble this season."

I couldn't see anyone, but I felt Thomas' presence. Speaking in the direction where I sensed he stood, I thanked him for preventing my fall. I said it had been my pleasure to keep Clara occupied.

I felt a light kiss on my cheek and heard a quiet voice, "It's delightful to finally meet you. Your friendship means a lot to Clara." Then I knew he was gone.

Clara's eyes were bright, and she had a big smile. "I was so afraid you and Thomas wouldn't get to meet. I'm so glad it finally happened!"

Meeting Thomas had made me temporarily forget everything else, but then I remembered the men we had just seen. I had a lot of questions.

Fortunately, Clara seemed to have gotten the information she needed, so all I had to do was listen. "Al started coming down here in 1925. He had just taken over as head of the crime syndicate in Chicago, so that first year he hadn't gained notoriety. He never stayed long; he would just come and go. All we knew about him at first was that he and Babe were friends, and he worked in Chicago. To me he seemed like a polite young man, but I had a distinct feeling I didn't want to get on his bad side. It wasn't long, though, before we started reading stories about Al Capone in the news. We found it hard to believe they had any connection to the young man we knew.

"Once Al became a nationally-known figure, people began to speculate about why he had come to St. Petersburg. Everyone had an opinion. I believed it was a combination of several things. I think he came because he liked the area and the weather, he had friends here, and he had fun.

"Al liked it here enough that he began to buy property. Some people swore he didn't owned anything in this area because his name was never found on a deed. That's true. Al rarely bought anything in his own name; instead he bought property through a corporation that he and some friends set up. For their own protection, they made it very difficult for anyone to be able to find out who actually owned the corporation.

"Al bought quite a bit of land in the St. Petersburg-Gulfport area. Legend says he was the one who donated the land to the American Legion for their children's hospital. That wouldn't surprise me at all because Babe Ruth gave money to help get the hospital started. Al could be very generous, and giving land for a children's hospital that his friend supported was absolutely something he would do.

"Al enjoyed the Gangplank and spent a lot of time there when he came to town. We were amused when we heard a rumor had spread that Al owned a share in it. Part of the proof offered for his involvement with the nightclub seemed to be that he didn't start coming to St. Petersburg until after the Gangplank had been built. That was true, as was the fact that the Yankees and Babe Ruth started spring training here that same year.

"It was hinted that Walter P. didn't have trouble getting booze because Al got it for him. We all knew Walter P. had never had any trouble getting liquor. He knew where to get the good stuff and he didn't need a mobster from Chicago to help him.

"Some people even claimed the only way the Gangplank got big name entertainers was because of Al's help. Honestly, it wasn't hard to get entertainers to come to Florida in the winter, especially if you paid well, which Walter P. did. Anyway, people like Duke Ellington and Count Basie came from New York not Chicago.

"People tried to connect Al and Walter P. any way they could. They pointed out that Al and his men always used Walter P.'s airfield when they came to St. Petersburg, but so did a lot of people. It was a nice airfield. They talked about how much time Al spent at the Gangplank. We all spent a lot of time there! It had the best liquor and entertainment in town. Some people even swore Al stayed at the Jungle Hotel when he came down. His men stayed there but Al never did. He preferred to stay at the Vinoy or the Don CeSar.

"I doubted Al's ownership in the Gangplank. As far as I knew, Walter P. didn't even know him when the speakeasy was built. I couldn't imagine Walter P. taking on a partner and share the profits in a successful business. It did happen to be the type of story, though, that would bring people to the speakeasy in hopes of seeing a famous gangster. I wouldn't have been at all surprised to find the story originated with Walter P.

"It might have been possible that Al owned part of the Gangplank after the stock market crashed in 1929. Walter P. lost everything else, but he did hold on to the Gangplank for a couple of years with loans and help from friends. Al might have stepped in then, but I doubt it because that was when he started having big problems of his own.

"The FBI had been watching Al, trying to find something they could use to remove him from power. They had a difficult time because he was so popular in Chicago. The press liked him and so did the people; no one wanted to do anything to intentionally cause him harm.

"Then in 1929, the Valentine's Day massacre took place. Several men belonging to a faction challenging Al for control of Chicago were killed. When the massacre happened Al was vacationing at his estate on Palm Island near

Miami Beach. While it would have been impossible for him to have been directly involved in the murders, the belief was widely held that he ordered the killings. The FBI searched long and hard but could not find any proof that Al was involved in the crime. Frustrated, they finally arrested him on the charge of carrying a concealed weapon, and sent him to jail for nine months.

"After Al's release they put him on trial for tax evasion. Prohibition had been good for Al. His income that year had been estimated to be around sixty million dollars! Unfortunately, he hadn't paid income tax on any of it. The jury only took a few hours to find him guilty and send him to Alcatraz.

"After serving eight years of his sentence Al was released. He was suffering from the complications of syphilis and had severe dementia. His health had deteriorated to the point where they no longer considered him a threat to anyone. He lived the rest of his life as a recluse at his estate on Palm Island.

"Al still comes back to the Gangplank now and then. I think he likes to come because here he is just Al and not Al Capone.

Lou Gehrig and Babe Ruth with an admirer in St. Petersburg, 1934

Photo from the St. Petersburg Museum of History

Today I consider myself the luckiest man on the face of the earth… I might have been given a bad break, but I've got an awful lot to live for.

LOU GEHRIG

Lou Gehrig

"Baseball helped this area make it through the Depression," Clara said as we walked. "In 1929, there were ten major league teams holding their spring training within fifty miles of St. Petersburg. Teams, including their players, managers, and staff, might require at least a hundred rooms while they were here. Fortunately, no matter how bad times were, some fans still came to watch their team. That kept tourism alive and hotels and restaurants in business.

"The Phillies had moved their spring training to Winter Haven. So when the Yankees started coming down in 1925, Thomas and I didn't feel disloyal about riding the trolley into town to watch them play. Games were played on Monday and Wednesday afternoons. If we got there late, all the twenty-five cent general admission seats would be gone, and we would have to pay a dollar for a box seat. Even people who had no interest in baseball came to the games. They wanted to be able to say they had seen Babe Ruth and Lou Gehrig play. Stores and businesses closed during game times so their employees could watch the best known team in baseball."

Lou Gehrig! I wondered if Clara knew him, too. Marie said she had met almost everyone. Clara shook her head no. "I talked to him several times, but I didn't really know him. He and Thomas were friends, but Lou was a very private man and felt uncomfortable around people."

Something I heard in Clara's voice made me wonder if she hadn't liked the ballplayer. "Oh, I did like Lou," she said, "but I didn't care for his mother! Christina Gehrig might win the award for the most obnoxious person I have ever met. We all tried to avoid her. She started every conversation with who her son was and what he did, like we hadn't heard of Lou Gehrig. It always annoyed me that she never considered baseball her son's career. She believed when Lou finally got tired of playing ball he would turn to the career she had chosen for him, engineering."

We reached the park and saw the tea table by our usual bench. We had been walking for quite a while, and I sat down with relief. Clara poured the tea. I gratefully took a cup. After a few sips she went back to her story. "One of the things about staying in a hotel like the Sunset was that there was always someone who knows something about anyone of importance. While the Gehrigs were definitely not in the same social class as guests at the Sunset, several of the residents knew a great deal about them and were eager to share their knowledge.

"Lou's parents, Heinrich and Christina, settled in Manhattan when they emigrated from Germany. Unfortunately, America did not turn out to be a land of opportunity for them. Heinrich was an alcoholic and couldn't keep a job so taking care of the family fell on Christina. She worked two jobs at a time just to provide for their basic needs. Three of her four children died in infancy and the losses almost destroyed her. Lou became her reason for living.

"Boys in the Gehrigs' neighborhood went to work when they finished elementary school, but Christina wanted her son to get an education. Lou did well in high school, but he also found a new interest, sports. Christina found that disturbing; sports did not fit into the plans she had for her son.

"One of Lou's college coaches, a delightful gentleman we called Homer, used to stay at the Sunset. He had retired and liked to come down to watch his former protégé during spring training. He didn't care for Christina and wasn't hesitant to tell people. He related how she tried to keep her son from playing baseball by insisting Lou turn down the sports scholarship he received from Columbia University. She insisted her son was not going to college to play games; he was going to become an engineer."

Clara stopped and took a sip of her tea. Smiling she continued, "I have a feeling Christina met her match in Homer. His determination that Lou accept the scholarship was as strong as Christina's that it be turned down. Homer recognized that Lou's natural talent and self-discipline meant he could become a great athlete; if he had the right coach. Christina finally had to accept that she could not afford to send Lou to college without the scholarship, but she insisted that he enroll in engineering courses.

"Lou turned out to be everything Homer had hoped. They developed a father-son relationship and the athlete looked to his coach for advice. Christina got sick during her son's sophomore year in college, and the job of taking care of the family fell to Lou. He saw no option other than dropping out of school and going to work. Homer knew if that happened the young man would never play baseball. The coach spoke with some of the scouts who had been watching his protégé and a few days later Lou received an offer to play for the New York Yankees.

"The contract was what Lou had always dreamed of, and Homer suggested he sign it immediately. Lou refused. He wanted to take the offer home to show his mother." Clara took another sip of tea, "I remember Homer shaking his head as he told us that everyone knew that Christina would not like the idea of her son playing professional baseball. To Lou's shock, he found his mother didn't care about his dreams, or that the money being offered would make life easy for them. She ordered him to stay in school and become an engineer.

"Lou had always done what his mother wanted, but this time he had to make the decision that he knew was right. They had no money for him to stay in school, and he had no interest in being an engineer. He wanted to play for the Yankees. This opportunity would come only once and he wasn't going to turn it down. Lou asked Homer to go with him when he signed the contract."

Clara chuckled, "I guess Christina couldn't believe it when she learned what her son had done. She made everyone's life miserable for a while, especially Homer's. However, Christina soon found there were unexpected benefits to Lou's decision. No one had ever paid any attention to the lowly German laundress before, but she suddenly had reporters asking to interview her and photographers taking her picture. She became the center of attention and she loved it!"

Sitting back, Clara's smile grew bigger. "I wish you could have heard Babe tell about the first time he met Christina. He had gone to the Gehrigs' house to walk to practice with Lou. When he rang the doorbell he saw a woman standing inside with an apron on and a broom in one hand, but she refused to come to the door. He heard her saying 'riese' which is German for giant. Babe stood at six feet two inches, and he knew he was tall. He was about seven inches taller than the average man, but he found it amusing to hear this woman calling him a giant.

"Babe kept ringing the bell and finally Christina asked, in German, who was there. She had found that using her native language usually insured the person at the door would leave. To her surprise the giant answered in perfect German. He told her to tell Lou that Babe Ruth had come to walk to practice with him. Christina, being her usual charming self, informed him that 'Babe' was not a man's name and demanded to know his real name. Laughing, he gave his full name, George Herman Ruth, Junior.

"Christina never referred to Babe as anything but George. That confused a lot of people because with her accent it came out 'Jidge.' Often, after she left a room, someone would ask who the Judge was that she kept talking about.

"Even though Christina could be difficult, Babe treasured the time he spent with the Gehrigs. He told me it was the only home he ever had. He and Lou walked to practice together, and they liked being with each other. They quickly became best friends."

Clara's smile disappeared, "Lou met Eleanor Twitchell, a lovely young woman from a well-to-do family in Chicago, at a party. She and the ballplayer were complete opposites in most ways, but they were attracted to each other. Christina had been successful in chasing off any young woman Lou had shown an interest in, so he decided his mother wouldn't learn about Eleanor.

"Christina didn't find out about the courtship until they announced their engagement, and she was livid! Lou wanted his mother's approval for the marriage, but she refused to give it and did everything she could to break up the couple. A few days before the wedding Lou finally had enough of his mother's hysterics. He asked Eleanor if she would be willing to get married right then, and she agreed. Lou called the mayor and asked him to come over and perform the nuptials. The wedding took place in the couple's new apartment. It was a small, quiet, peaceful ceremony, without Christina. The newlyweds were escorted to the afternoon game by the mayor's motorcade."

"Once Lou was married, life began to change for his parents. I got to watch one of the changes first hand. While Lou and Eleanor never stayed at the Sunset, Eleanor liked to come here for tea. She and I had a lot in common. We became good friends and spent quite a bit of time together.

"Christina had always stayed with Lou when he came down for spring training. She considered that her right as his mother. However, once Lou got married his wife decided that needed to change. When Lou informed his parents they would have to get their own apartment his mother refused. Marriage did not change her rights. To her shock, when she and Heinrich showed up with their suitcases, Eleanor would not let them in the apartment. She told them that they had reservations at the Sunset Hotel and shut the door.

"Eleanor had told me what she was going to do, so I had a seat by the reception desk where I could see and hear everything when the Gehrigs arrived. Christina was irate. She loudly informed everyone that her son would be horrified when he learned what 'that woman' had done. She announced she would only be here a short time; her son needed her closer to him. She made such a scene that the manager finally had to take her into his office to calm her down. No one seemed to care when they moved out a few days later."

Clara looked out over the Bay before continuing, "Christina liked Babe, but she resented his talent and popularity. She felt her son wasn't being treated fairly by the team." I heard a hint of anger in Clara's voice. "This is one time I have to agree with Christina. They didn't treat Lou right! When contracts were signed that year, Babe's was for forty thousand dollars while Lou got only eight thousand! The management knew Lou would accept anything they offered, and they also knew Babe loved negotiating. They took advantage of Lou's reticence. Christina was furious, but instead of talking to the Yankee's management she took her anger out on Babe and his family.

"Claire Ruth was, at the same time, starting to have concerns. Babe's lifestyle had begun affecting his game. Claire realized Lou's discipline, hard work, and dedication were paying off. Lou was playing well and Babe was not. Claire feared Lou would take the top spot on the team, and that spot belonged to her husband! She started her own vendetta against Lou and the Gehrigs.

"As time went on the situation continued to worsen. Things were said, accusations made, and the two women demanded that the men cut off all contact with each other. Sadly, neither Lou nor Babe had the courage to stand up to the women. As a result, both men lost their best friend.

"Claire's fears were prophetic. The following year Babe was dropped from the Yankees. Lou became the team leader and got the attention his mother had always wanted for him. He hated every minute of it!"

Clara took another sip of tea, and I noticed when she sat her cup down that her hand was shaking. "A couple of years later, Thomas mentioned to me that he didn't think Lou seemed to be running as fast or hitting as hard as he normally did. I hadn't noticed anything and thought Thomas had to be imagining things, but the next year during spring training even I could see something was wrong. I invited Eleanor over for tea and asked about Lou. She seemed relieved to talk about his problems. She said Lou was in constant pain and having trouble with his coordination. He had been to several doctors, but they had no idea what could be wrong. His symptoms were getting worse. She had an appointment for him to go to the Mayo Clinic as soon as he finished spring training.

"The diagnosis from the Clinic was much worse than anything Eleanor had anticipated. Lou had ALS, amyotrophic lateral sclerosis. His motor neurons were dying and his brain was losing the ability to control his muscles. He retired from baseball immediately.

"Eleanor called to tell me about the test results. She said they would be honoring Lou at the Yankees' game on July 4th and asked if we could come. Of course we went! Babe also returned for the ceremony. I cried when he and

Lou hugged. I don't know what they said to each other, but it was the first time they had spoken in five years.

"Nothing could be done for Lou. He tried to stay as active as he could, but life got harder and harder each day. He died two years later at the age of thirty-seven."

Clara wiped away a tear. "Lou's death hit us all hard. I'm glad he got the chance to do what he loved. He and Babe were teammates and best friends for many years. They had so much in common, but strong athletes can be weak men. Lou and Babe allowed their weaknesses to destroy one of the most valuable things they had in life, their friendship."

How can you relax in a world where "truffle" can mean either chocolate of fungus?

DAN PIRARO

Crab Stuffed Mushrooms with Parmesan
John Rivard-Chef Crystal Bay Hotel
1 lb. large mushrooms (about 2 inches across)
7 oz. crab meat   5 green onions thinly sliced
¼ tsp. dried thyme   ¼ tsp. dried oregano
¼ tsp. savory black pepper   ¼ cup grated Parmesan cheese
1/3 cup mayonnaise   ¼ tsp. paprika

Wipe mushrooms clean with a damp towel. Remove the stems and gills making a deep cup. In a medium bowl combine crabmeat, green onions, herbs and pepper. Mix in mayo and ¼ c. of Parmesan until well combined. (Refrigerate mixture if you do not use it immediately.) Fill mushrooms with rounded teaspoons of filling and place them in an ungreased baking dish. Sprinkle tops with Parmesan cheese and paprika. Bake at 350° for 15 minutes. Remove from oven and serve immediately.

Inspired by The Great Gatsby

Babe Ruth and two young fans in St. Petersburg

Photo from the St. Petersburg Museum of History

Never let the fear of striking out keep you from playing the game.

BABE RUTH

Babe Ruth

I loved listening to Clara tell about people she knew, and I was curious to hear what she had to say about Babe Ruth. To be truthful, I realized I didn't know much about him other than he played for the Yankees and he had been a good player. I had no idea what position he played or why he was such a legend in baseball.

Clara startled me by breaking into my thoughts with a huff. "How could you not know about Babe Ruth? No one would refer to him as just a 'good' player, he was considered to be one of the greatest players in baseball! He played outfield and he hit over 700 homeruns. That record stood for forty years! That's why he is a legend."

Obviously my ignorance had upset Clara. I apologized and told her I would like to know more about him. Clara sighed, "I'm sorry I reacted so strongly. It just seemed impossible to me that you wouldn't know more. We read about Babe every day in the papers. We talked about how he played, how many runs he batted in, and how many home runs he hit. I find it hard to remember that he is no longer in the daily news, and there is no reason why you would know about him."

I could hear admiration in Clara's voice as she continued. "There is so much to tell that I hardly know where to start. I guess what comes to my mind first is how much Babe enjoyed people. It didn't make any difference if they were black, white, young, old, rich, poor, or even if they were a fan of his or not, he just liked being with people. He loved children and never failed to sign autographs for them. He also had a special place in his heart for the elderly. When he heard about a local woman celebrating her 104th birthday he decided to take her a huge bouquet of roses. She had no idea who Babe Ruth was, but she loved the roses and the attention she got when he delivered them.

"Babe enjoyed his time down here each winter. He would go to the barber shop every morning for a shave and to share jokes with anyone who happened to be there. He said fishing relaxed him, so he'd go out on Boca Ciega Bay in the mornings hoping to catch a grouper or mackerel. If he caught something he'd bring it to the chefs at the Sunset and ask them to fix it for his supper.

"Even though at least half the country idolized him, Babe looked at himself as an ordinary person. He walked to work and loved unhealthy food, especially hot dogs. He liked flashy clothes and drove his convertible with the top down so he could wave at people. He just seemed to be a big kid enjoying life.

"Babe didn't have a lot of education, but he wasn't dumb. I remember when Carl Sandburg came down to interview him. Mr. Sandburg pompously stated that the two greatest works ever written were the Bible and Shakespeare. Knowing the baseball player had received only the barest education at the orphanage, the poet asked which parts of those works Babe liked. I doubt Babe ever read a word of Shakespeare in his life, but being raised at St. Mary's meant he had to know the Bible. He could have answered the question if he had wanted, but he looked at Mr. Sandburg as though the poet had lost his mind and said, 'Baseball players don't have time to read!'

Clara paused, and when she spoke again her voice held a somber note. "People envied Babe but his life had not always been easy. Today most people have access to medical care, so it is hard to remember that in the late 1800's few people had that luxury. Almost every family lost at least one child, and out of the Ruth's eight children only George Jr. and a sister survived."

George Jr? It took me a few seconds to remember that Babe's real name was George Herman Ruth Jr.

"His parents owned a tavern in Baltimore and they spent all their time running it. I would have thought with having lost six children the Ruths would pay some attention to their surviving offspring, but they didn't. George Jr. had to raise himself and he didn't do it very well. Fortunately in 1902, when Babe was seven, the state stepped in sent him to St. Mary's, an orphanage/boarding school for troubled boys." Clara's voice hardened, "The Ruth's attitude toward their children is unfathomable to me, because once their son went to St. Mary's they forgot about him! That school became his home for the next twelve years.

"The priests at the orphanage taught the boys to play baseball, and they realized George Jr. was a talented player. When he turned nineteen, one of the priests contacted the manager of a minor league team and asked him to come and watch their ward play. The manager recognized the young man's ability and immediately offered him a contract. Babe told us the offer shocked him. He loved playing ball more than anything, and he knew he played well, but he had no idea how well.

"He wanted to sign the contract right then but there was a problem. At nineteen the state considered him a minor, and the agreement had to be signed by his guardian. He didn't have one! The manager, realizing the young man had great potential, got himself appointed as the guardian and signed the contract." Clara paused for a moment, "If that manager hadn't been willing to take a chance on a penniless ward of the state, no one would have ever heard of Babe Ruth. What a loss that would have been!

"When Babe got the contract he thought he had it made. However, life outside of St. Mary's turned out to be much more difficult than he anticipated. Discipline had been very strict in the orphanage. The boys were told what to do, when to do it, and they were expected to obey without questioning. George Jr. went from a world where there were no options to a world with nothing but options. He had no idea how to exist in his new universe!"

This had been interesting, but Clara had ignored one of the things I wanted to know. Where did the name 'Babe' come from? My first guess would have been a family nickname, but that didn't seem possible since he hadn't had a family. I wondered if he could have gotten it at the orphanage, but I had a feeling that wasn't right either. Clara obviously wanted me to ask, so I did.

"Well," Clara replied, "he didn't get the name until he started playing baseball. George Jr. realized he needed a lot of help learning about life. The only person he felt he could trust was the manager who had signed as his guardian. He followed him everywhere, asking questions and watching how he did things. The other members of the team didn't understand what was going on. They began laughing about the manager's new 'babe.' The name stuck, but Babe got the last laugh. He didn't stay a 'babe' for long as far as playing baseball went. In a couple of months he was called up to play for the Boston Red Sox.

"Not long after he moved to Boston, Babe met Helen, a waitress at the coffee shop where he had breakfast each morning. They were both young, on their own, and lonely. They were attracted to each other and decided it would be easier to face the world together than alone, so they got married.

"Babe and Helen loved children and hoped to have a large family. After a few years they realized that wasn't going to happen, and Babe suggested they adopt a child. The agency offered them a newborn girl and they were ecstatic. They named their new daughter Dorothy. Helen told me she fell in love with the little girl the minute she saw her. She said that becoming a family was the happiest time in their marriage. Unfortunately, the happy time didn't last.

"Babe was traded to the New York Yankees, and Helen quickly found her husband had a serious flaw where marriage was concerned—unfaithfulness. He couldn't resist a willing woman. Helen said she could overlook a lot of things, but she refused to overlook infidelity. Babe, away from home much of the time with training and games, quickly discovered there were a lot of willing women. He tried to take advantage of every opportunity that presented herself.

"Devastated by what was happening, Helen had one more shock coming. She learned what many people already knew; their daughter was actually Babe's child by one of his mistresses! Helen didn't know what to do or where to turn. She thought about giving up the little girl, but she realized she loved her daughter too much to do that. She decided if she had to give up someone it would be her husband, not Dorothy."

Clara picked up the teapot and tried to pour another cup, but it was empty. She took off the lid and looked inside, I guess to make sure there wasn't any tea hiding anywhere. Sighing she set the pot down. Since the tea was gone Clara suggested that we walk, so we headed toward the Bay. "The year the Yankees started coming here for spring training was not a good time for Babe. We had heard the talk about his drinking and womanizing, but we thought it was just gossip and didn't pay any attention to it. The team management, however, knew the truth and insisted that Babe and Helen try to reconcile during spring training. The team rented an apartment for the Ruths at the Sunset, and Helen and Dorothy came down to be with Babe."

We walked quietly for a bit. Then Clara said, "Helen and I were almost the same age, and I liked her immediately. She wasn't polished, but she was attractive, friendly, and down to earth. All the attention she got as Babe Ruth's wife made her uncomfortable, and she did her best to protect their daughter from exploitation. Helen cared for Babe and she hoped they would be able to put the marriage back together, but being realistic she had doubts. Sadly, it didn't take long for her to see her husband had no intention of changing his ways. Heartbroken, she and Dorothy returned home." Clara sighed, "I never saw Helen again after she left. She moved to Massachusetts and died in a house fire a couple of years later. Her death saddened me because she was so young and full of dreams for her daughter and herself.

"Babe continued to stay at the Sunset that year. Thomas and I got along with him, but most of the residents did not look at his presence positively. Babe liked to have a good time, and there were many horrified gasps when he led one young woman after another, sometimes on the same night, up to his room."

We were walking down Sunset Drive when Clara stopped in front of a large, beautiful, two-story, brick home. "The next year Babe moved into this house. He gave some great parties here. Some people thought Babe had purchased the home, but the owner told me he loaned it to Babe for spring training. He wanted to be able to say he lived in a house where Babe Ruth had lived."

I had to smile. It seems some things don't change. There was a "for sale" sign in the front yard and I had seen an advertisement for the house in the newspaper. The ad proudly proclaimed that the home had once belonged to Babe Ruth.

On our way back to the Sunset Clara continued, "The following year Babe and Lou moved downtown into the two penthouses at the Flori-de-Leon.

It was the perfect arrangement for them. As neighbors they still walked to practice together, but they each had their own separate space. Lou, being painfully shy, had a private elevator installed that only went to his penthouse. He didn't want to run into fans and have to make small talk. Babe, on the other hand, loved riding the elevator just to see who he could meet.

"After Helen's death Babe was free to marry again, and he wed quickly. He had fallen in love with an actress named Claire Hodgson and their wedding took place at dawn in St. Gregory's Catholic Church in New York City. The ceremony had to be early because it was opening day of the 1929 baseball season, and Babe had to be on time for the game. Like Lou, Babe never let a wedding get in the way of baseball."

Clara hesitated for a moment, "I probably shouldn't say it, but I never really cared for Babe's second wife. She enjoyed being Mrs. Babe Ruth and loved being the center of attention. She insisted that Babe adopt her twelve-year-old daughter, Julia, as soon as they were married. Julia took after her mother in loving the limelight, and she always introduced herself as Babe Ruth's daughter.

"Claire got an unwelcome surprise shortly after their wedding. She learned that Babe's five year-old daughter, Dorothy, would be coming to live with them. Claire didn't want the little girl and tried to get Babe to put her up for adoption, but he refused. Claire always resented Dorothy. I know the little girl did not have an easy life.

Babe on the golf course in St. Petersburg 1932
Photo from the St. Petersburg Museum of History

"Babe's unbridled lifestyle began to take its toll as time went on. His hitting and fielding were not what they once were. He had hoped to manage a team once he stopped playing baseball, but his excesses weren't what owners looked for in a manager. They felt that a man who couldn't manage himself wouldn't be able to manage a team. The Yankees refused to renew his contract in 1935, and Babe quit baseball.

"He and Claire bought a home here and came down regularly during the winter season. Golf became his main interest, but he found much of his joy in life disappeared without baseball. His health continued to deteriorate, and in 1948 the whole nation grieved when we learned that he had died of throat cancer at the age of fifty-three."

Clara paused and with solemnness that I rarely heard said, "Babe and Lou were two men I feel fortunate to have met. They were idolized by the public but they weren't perfect. They both had flaws. Those flaws kept them from being gods and made them men we could connect with and feel like we knew."

The Sunset Hotel, 1939
Photo from the St. Petersburg Museum of History

Good friends are like stars. You don't always see them, but you always know they're there!

ANONYMOUS

Life Goes On

Clara was not in a good mood when we met the next time. Work had started in earnest at the hotel. She complained about the noise and maintained they should have waited until the end of season to start construction. "That's the way it's done!" she snapped, "They wait until we leave so they don't inconvenience anyone."

She told me that the library had been turned into an office. A combination lock had been installed on the door to keep intruders out. It didn't stop Clara and her friends from using the room, and to their delight they found any time they went in or out of the library the lock on the door swayed. Everyone started making regular trips to the room. Some of the workers found it very disconcerting to see the lock suddenly start swinging for no apparent reason.

Clara learned the building was to become a holistic health center, where people would come for alternative healing and to learn how to live their lives to the fullest. She also heard they were planning to restore the hotel to its original condition. Nothing would please her more than having the Sunset returned to the wonderful place she once knew, but she didn't want to get too hopeful. Previous owners had promised to renovate the building before, but no one had ever followed through.

The building and grounds looked so bad that I wondered if it would even be possible to restore them. Clara shook her head, "It's so sad to see the Sunset looking this way. It has been let go before, but it's never been this bad."

Hoping to take Clara's mind off the conditions at the hotel, I asked her to tell me what happened in the 1930s. "Well, it took several years for things to get back to normal," she said. "Walter P. had never known hard times to last more than a year or two, and he had difficulty accepting that things had permanently changed.

He decided to get 1931 started off right by throwing a big party. His uncle had taken over the Jungle, but Walter P. still had an active role in managing the hotel. He invited two hundred and fifty guests to his New Year's Eve Snowball Ball. You can't imagine our excitement about the idea of one of Walter P.'s parties again!

"When we arrived at the Jungle we discovered the dining room had been transformed into a forest. The walls were lined with pine and cedar trees sparkling with snow. Puffy white clouds covered the ceiling and snowmen stood everywhere. A huge clock hung from the center of the room, and under it sat a very large snowman.

"Supper started at 10 p.m. with dancing and music between each course. We all kept a close eye on the time. Just as the clock reached midnight, Walter P. struck the large snowman. Its head had been filled with melodious bells and their tones welcomed in 1931. As we cheered in the

New Year the lights went out; we were instructed to turn on the miniature flashlights we had been given when we arrived. The flashlights, and the sparkle they created on snow in the trees and sky, illuminated the first dance of the New Year.

"The best part of the evening was still to come. Everyone was ushered outside to an unbelievable sight. Walter P. had brought in one thousand snowballs! We had a snowball fight; men against the women. The weather was cool and the snowballs lasted for quite a while. That party is one of my favorite memories.

"Things had been solemn for so long that we found it a relief to have fun. We hoped that Walter P. would be correct and this year would prove to be the end of the hard times. Unfortunately, he wasn't. Things eventually got better, but the lifestyle we loved so much never returned. We now knew that you couldn't sit on the top of the world forever. Eventually you were going to fall off, and when you did it hurt.

"Thomas and I tried to live our lives as normally as we could. Most of our friends were still here and we continued to stay at the Sunset. We ate at restaurants, went into town, played golf, and attended ballgames, but it was not the same. We still went to the Gangplank, but even that was doomed. The speakeasy closed its doors long before Prohibition ended in December of 1933.

"Things were changing everywhere. There were many new faces at the Sunset. Some people who had been coming for years lost their money when the market crashed, and could no longer return. Others had gotten too old to make the trip. Those of us who could still come had started altering the ways we did things. Hardly anyone traveled by train anymore; we all drove. We liked the freedom a car gave us, but traveling by automobile meant we were limited in what we could bring.

"The Sunset's owners saw the trends and began making modifications. They built a garage across the street where guests could keep their cars. They knew the people who arrived by automobile would no longer want big, unfurnished rooms. So over the off-season they began dividing the apartments into suites. Each suite was nice sized and exquisitely furnished. No one could complain about a lack of comfort or not having enough room. When they finished the renovation, the hotel had seventy furnished suites instead of the original thirty units."

A table appeared and Clara paused while we drank a cup of tea. Then she continued, "Many of the people who drove liked to arrive by the first of December. They wanted to be here before the weather and roads got too bad up north. Hotels fought having to open that early, but they finally had to give in to demand. By the middle of the 1930's most hotels here were open by the first of December.

The Sunset Hotel in 1940
Photo from St. Petersburg Museum of History

"It took the Sunset a few years to recover from the Depression. The hotel stayed fairly full in the early 1930's, but there were always rooms available. You could stay in a single room for five dollars a night without meals, or for nine dollars with meals. A double room cost twice as much as a single.

"By 1935, things were definitely turning around. That was the year St. Petersburg began decorating for Christmas. They put up colored electric lights along the streets and in the parks. The Sunset, again, had been sold. When we arrived that year, to our delight we found the hotel had been totally renovated! The main entrance had been redone and moved from Central Avenue to 74th Street. A glassed-in sun porch had been added along the north wing of the building, and that was a well-appreciated upgrade. The new steam heat and hot water systems insured rooms stayed warm and the water hot.

"The new owners got into the spirit of the season and covered the building and grounds with lights. The inside of the hotel was beautifully decorated for the holidays with trees everywhere. For the first time in years there were no empty rooms! Every room was filled with guests, children, and grandchildren who came down for the holidays. The Sunset had so many advanced bookings it had to open early to accommodate everyone. The hotel again became the place to stay.

"The staff and help at the Sunset had always been excellent. The management, knowing good service played a big part in any hotel's success, wanted to keep it that way. The help, which included the maids, waiters, cooks, and maintenance people, stayed in the hotel dormitories over the laundry and garages. Those quarters had been remodeled and repainted. The hotel's fulltime staff: a social director, a housekeeper, a dining room hostess, the couple in charge of the front desk, plus the two couples who owned and managed the Sunset, lived at the hotel or in houses on the hotel property.

"The social director at the hotel did a wonderful job! Events were open to all guests and to the Pasadena neighborhood. We had weekly card parties, bridge tournaments, and bingo games. There were community sings, plays, dance troops, vocalists, lectures, and once a season there was a large theatrical production. Events were well attended. There was seldom an evening when something wasn't going on in either the west lounge or the main lounge, and often both were in use.

"Activities weren't limited to programs at the hotel. We had tennis and golf tournaments, plus fishing contests. The National Shuffleboard champions even came once and played exhibitions for us!"

While many of the activities sounded like fun, I couldn't think of anything that sounded less interesting than a shuffleboard exhibition. Evidently, Clara could. Glaring at me she snapped, "We all enjoyed that very much! We found it exciting to watch."

Clara obviously felt strongly about shuffleboard because it took her a bit to continue. "We went on lots of boat trips. We would go to Tarpon Springs for the day, the Belleview Biltmore for lunch, or even deep sea fishing. We would go to baseball games, the dog races, and on picnics. There was never a shortage of anything to do.

"Season always opened with a big Christmas party. They would decorate the hotel beautifully and put up trees in the lounges and on the lawn. Santa came and we had a gift exchange followed by a carol sing. Dinner and dancing ended the evening. The last big party of the season was the St. Patrick's Day Party, which always had special entertainment.

"Walter P. lost the Gangplank and the Jungle Prado in 1931. The people who bought the Jungle Prado, to Walter P.'s horror, turned the building into a lodge which they called The Chimney. The whole building was converted into apartments, and the Gangplank, where we had so many delightful times, disappeared forever. Cottages, marketed to families with children, were built on the grounds. Enough units were added that the kitchen and dining room could no longer accommodate the number of people staying there. The proprietors had no more money to put into the lodge for improvements, so they had to put it up for sale.

"The Sunset's owners liked the housing diversity that the lodge and cottages offered, so they purchased the complex at the end of February. In order to have things ready for the next season they began to make changes immediately. The kitchen and dining facilities at The Chimney were closed. That meant for the final month of season people from the lodge and cottages came to the Sunset for their meals.

"Children in the dining room certainly livened things up for a while! The guests from the lodge were allowed to take part in our activities, attend programs we had, and use the library and shuffleboard courts. That did not go over well with many of the residents at the hotel. I enjoyed the freshness that the people from The Chimney brought, but I have to admit I was glad to know it wouldn't be forever.

"A new craze which was supposed to be very healthy had started to become popular, it was called sunbathing. At first I found it quite shocking to see women with brown arms, legs, and faces, but I quickly got used to it. I enjoyed sunbathing, but most of the older women at the Sunset found it scandalous, and they were not happy when the hotel added sunbathing cabanas in 1939.

"In the 1940's things changed again when the United States entered the war in Europe. The government imposed travel restrictions and gas and food rationings. The hotels again sat empty. St. Petersburg's leaders decided all those vacant rooms could be used as military housing, so they petitioned for a military base to be located here. The petition was granted and the Technical Service Training Center for the Army Air Corps moved to St. Petersburg. Over one hundred thousand soldiers trained here. All the major hotels and most of the smaller ones were leased by the military to house the soldiers.

1943 Military Parade on Central Avenue
Photo from the St. Petersburg Museum of History

"After the War, when we were able to return again, we found things around the Sunset had changed. The area was no longer the quiet, out of the way place it had always been. Thomas had begun thinking about retirement, and we wanted a place where we could relax. We had begun flying down instead of driving, so we could bring very little with us, other than clothes. We hoped to spend more time in Florida; however, the Sunset was still open only a few months each year. We wanted to see how we liked being here at various times of the year, so Thomas and I began to look at buying our own place.

"Several of our friends were buying apartments. They especially liked the ones being built on the islands just across Boca Ciega Bay. Those apartments were right on the water with beautiful views, and it was quiet. You could furnish your unit the way you liked, and you didn't have to bring anything when you came down. Many of the newer buildings even had air-conditioning! That meant you could be down here anytime and still be comfortable. We knew people who were coming down in early November and staying until May.

"Marie and Joseph sold their house in the Jungle and bought a large apartment in a new building on the beach. They had lots of windows and every convenience imaginable, including air-conditioning. The complex also had a swimming pool! We learned the unit next to them was available, so we bought it and moved to the beach. Our new apartment had splendid views of the Gulf, and it belonged to us.

"I have to admit I did miss the Sunset Hotel, and Marie and I often came over for lunch with friends. In the 1950's, we learned that the Sunset was going to become a residential hotel. It would be open year round, but it would be closed to the public. After almost forty years my time at the Sunset ended."

Clara sighed, "It seems like we've ended on a sad note, and the time has been anything but sad." We stood up and walked across the street. When we got to the walk leading to the hotel Clara gave me a hug. "Good-bye dear. I'll see you later." She walked up the steps and when she got to the door she turned and waved. Then she disappeared, and I went home.

The Crystal Bay Hotel, 2015
Photo courtesy of Mark Tong

This is a wonderful day. I've never seen this one before.

Maya Angelou

Crystal Bay

I saw the sea fog rolling in quickly as I started my walk. I had chosen to live on Boca Ciega Bay for the beautiful views, so for me the fog enhanced the beauty of the area. The cloudy wisps created a magical effect that muted sounds and quieted the world. The swirling mist almost seemed to be a portal that could open to times other than the present.

The heavy fog made it difficult for me to see even across the street, and it created a feeling of eeriness as familiar landmarks faded in and out of view. I had considered staying home, but I knew once I reached the old Sunset Hotel Clara would be waiting for me. She has a sixth sense about things and the fog would not be a problem for her. Walking with her is always a delight. She has been in this area for years and knows wonderful stories about its history and the people who have lived here.

I didn't see Clara when I arrived at the hotel. When she hadn't appeared after I walked around the building I decided to go back home. I didn't feel comfortable walking alone in the heavy fog.

The next day was beautiful. When I got to the park Clara wasn't there, but I saw the tea table with two cups so I knew she would be coming soon. I poured a cup of tea and sat back to wait. Hearing someone come up behind me I turned to greet Clara, but to my surprise Marie stood there. She asked if she could join me. I motioned for her to sit down and poured her a cup of tea.

We chatted about the weather and the work on the hotel. Finally, Marie set her cup down and looked at me, "Clara asked me to tell you goodbye. She and Thomas have gone home."

I sat there stunned! While I knew Clara had said they were only here for season, I didn't think she would leave this soon. She said season went through the end of March and they always had a big St. Patrick's Day party. It wasn't even the middle of March! Why had she left so soon?

"Clara had a hard time leaving," Marie said. "She has become very fond of you and felt like this would be the easiest way for her to go. She asked me to tell you how much she enjoyed sharing her memories with you. She hopes to see you again."

How could Clara just leave like this? We had so much more to talk about. When would she be back?

Marie tried to explain, "Almost all our friends have left. The noise at the hotel is constant and the workers are everywhere. There is no place where it is peaceful anymore. Clara and Thomas were among the last to go. Joseph and I will be leaving very soon. We will come back in October, but I don't know when Clara will be back. It depends on how soon they finish the work on the hotel. She usually comes back in December, but it is doubtful the renovations will be finished by then."

I set my cup down and stared out over the Bay. I couldn't imagine not seeing Clara for months! I had so much more I wanted know. I reached for my cup. Sadly, I realized the cup, the tea service, and Marie were all gone.

I kept a close watch on the hotel. There were cars and trucks parked around it, but I never saw anything being done. Finally, in late summer I got up the courage to go inside. Since I'd never been in the building I didn't know what to expect. The people working in the hotel were very friendly and welcoming. A woman volunteered to show me around and told me what they were doing. Floors and walls had been removed in some areas, the ceiling appeared to be mass of wires and pipes, and a gaping hole stood in one wall, which I learned had once been a fireplace. The only thing I could identify was a staircase. It stood in the middle of a large open area that my guide said had been the lobby and main lounge. I couldn't imagine what the hotel might have looked like when Clara lived there.

As I viewed the skeleton of what had once been a luxury hotel, I asked if they were tearing the building down or fixing it up. I was assured they were saving it. The woman explained that the building had to be stabilized before they could do any work. Part of the flooring had been removed by a previous owner and that had caused the building to shift. I knew they weren't going to be finished before season started.

I watched the building as the months went by. A lot of people came and went each day, but from the outside I couldn't see any progress being made. I needed to know how things were going, so I stopped in again. Walking through the door I could tell a lot had been done. The building now had floors, walls, and a completed fireplace. New window frames were being installed where they were needed. A worker proudly told me that they had kept as many of the original window panes as possible. I could easily spot the old glass panes as they rippled in the sunlight. The ceilings were still a mass of wires and pipes. They obviously had a long ways to go yet.

Finally, I saw work begin on the outside of the building! The hotel was repainted in a creamy yellow which I heard had been its original color. The wrought iron staircases were sanded down and painted. Wooden railings and trims were repaired or replaced. The swimming pool that had been partially installed a few years ago was being completed, and a privacy fence had been built around the pool.

Work continued on the building. It had been two years since Clara left and I felt the restoration had to be about done. I decided to stop in again. I paused in amazement when I walked through the doors. It looked like a 1920's luxury hotel. It felt quiet and peaceful. The lobby and main lounge, with their soothing cream walls, gave off an aura of a building that had started to feel proud again.

The original floors, made of heart of pine, gleamed in the main lounge. The carpet in the dining room and halls was a deep green with red roses. The dining room, which wasn't finished yet, had soft, foggy, gray walls; I could see how attractive it would eventually be. A demonstration kitchen stood at one end of the room. There guests would learn how to prepare meals that would help them maintain their best possible health.

We went upstairs to the guest accommodations. The walls had been painted in the same soft, foggy, gray as the dining room, but here the color seemed to change with the light making each suite look different. Most units had a sitting area and a bedroom but some had three rooms. There were sixty units in the building and they all looked inviting and comfortable. The work was coming to an end. The parking lot, where the old garages had once stood, was being resurfaced for a parking lot. The deck around the pool proudly sported new pavers. I hoped the hotel would meet with Clara's approval.

In October the hotel finally opened! It had been given a new name, the Crystal Bay. I worried about what Clara would think of that. I hadn't heard why it had been renamed, but I thought perhaps they wanted to give the building a fresh start.

They held an open house for the neighborhood and potential guests. I went, anxious to see the finished hotel. Walking up the steps I took a deep breath, opened the door, and walked in. A feeling of calmness came over me. A lovely wooden check-in desk stood to my right. It appeared to be an old apothecary chest, with healing herbs carved on the front. Comfortable-looking chairs and couches centered the fireplace.

The dining room had turned out to be as beautiful as I had imagined. The circular tables gave softness to the room, and each chair was cushioned in red with tiny palm trees woven into the fabric. A piano standing in the front corner of the room designated that area for entertainment or dancing. Going through the dining room I entered the west lounge which would be used for meditation and lectures. The porch on that side of the building had been enclosed many years ago to make a sun porch. Sunlight poured through the windows of what was now called the garden room; spa treatments would take place here.

I walked through the French doors that led out to the veranda where Clara and I had so often had tea. White wicker chairs invited guests to sit and relax. I found an empty seat and sat down. I looked out over the herb and butterfly garden. The brochure I picked up said the landscaping had been recreated from early pictures of the hotel. The palms swayed peacefully in the wind, and butterflies flitted serenely from one flower to another. I missed Clara and wished we could have shared the view.

The main lounge of the Crystal Bay 2015

Reception Desk 2015

Photos courtesy of Mark Tong

Going back into the hotel I went upstairs to look at the suites. The second floor had been designated as the Marilyn Monroe floor. Supposedly she had stayed at the hotel at some time. A large picture of her hung across from the elevator. It made me smile. I had no idea whether Marilyn had stayed here or not, but I knew Clara would have approved of fostering the idea that she had.

I enjoyed looking in the suites. Each had a tropical design but no two were the same. I noticed there were no telephones in any room. Today everyone has their own phone, and what was once a luxury is now no longer needed. Another interesting sign of the times was that the building had no televisions; however, internet was available.

The third floor was the Babe Ruth floor. A picture of him greeted guests when they stepped off the elevator. The last suite on the south wing is where Babe Ruth was supposed to have stayed. It was one of the larger suites. The sitting/writing room, surrounded by windows on three sides, looked out over the park and the bay. Clara had told me that was where Thomas' and Adeline's apartment had been when they came to the Sunset.

I hoped Clara would like the hotel; I thought it seemed lovely. Each area and room was welcoming and full of light. I wondered if I could come over some afternoon just to sit and relax in the soothing atmosphere. I knew, without a doubt, the building was very happy.

I looked for Clara as I wandered through the hotel, but I didn't see her. Refreshments were being served on the porch and people were being encouraged to have something to eat or drink and meet other guests. I walked out to the sun porch where they were serving. A plate of ginger cookies caught my eye! I had to have one. I took a bite and to my delight the cookie melted in my mouth. Tea was being poured and I accepted a cup. It surprised me to find it was an herbal tea. Not what I expected, but still delicious.

A lovely, stylishly dressed, young woman walked over and started talking to me. Something about her seemed vaguely familiar and I asked if we had met before. She said she didn't think so. She lived out of state and would be a guest at the hotel. She shared a hope that her stay at the Crystal Bay would help her achieve better health. I enjoyed talking with her and we found we had many interests in common.

Suddenly she leaned toward me and whispered, "I was one of the first to arrive! I couldn't wait to see what they had done with the hotel. Clara is going to love it, isn't she!"

Was this some kind of a joke? I looked at the young woman in shock. She smiled at me and winked. I knew I had seen that smile and wink before. Then I realized how I knew her. It was Adeline!

Why could I see her so easily now? Was it because Clara wasn't returning?

Adeline gave me a reassuring smile which made me feel as though we had been friends for a long time. She said she felt sure Clara would be back, but she was glad I could finally see her. She sounded so delighted. I knew we would be seeing each other again.

We talked a little longer and before we said goodbye we set a time to get together. I started home and had just reached the corner of the lot when I heard someone calling.

"There is no way I can keep up with you when you walk that fast. I am not as young as you are." I turned and saw Clara! She smiled, "It's so good to see you again! How do you like the hotel?"

I told her I thought they had done a wonderful job. Hesitantly, I asked how she liked it.

She nodded, "I have to agree with you, I felt at home the minute I walked through the door. I couldn't wait until December to find out what they had done. I am so glad I came! Thomas will be thrilled when he hears about it. He may want to come back a little earlier this year."

I told Clara that I had met Adeline but I hadn't seen anyone else. I asked if she thought others might return.

Clara looked surprised at my question, "I imagine everyone will be back. The hotel is so beautiful! I can't imagine anyone not wanting to return."

Laughing she said, "I guess you could call us the guests who refuse to leave."

Clara and MaryAnn having tea at the Crystal Bay Hotel, 2016

When it comes to the past, everyone writes fiction.

STEPHEN KING

Closing Thoughts

A large, old, white stucco building on the corner of Central Avenue and Park Street in St. Petersburg caught my interest the first time I saw it. I didn't know what it was, but I felt sure there had to be a story behind it. The edifice stood on a prime lot overlooking the Bay, and there was a 'for sale' sign in the yard. I knew it was probably doomed. Few people would have a use for something that old and big. Still, there was something about the structure that made me feel it would be a shame to lose it.

I started asking about the abandoned building. No one seemed to know much about it except that it was called the Sunset and at one time had been used as housing for older adults. I found out the property belonged to my friends, Mark and Lee Tong. They wanted to restore the building and turn it into a Wellness Center.

It seems the Sunset had had a varied life. It had opened as a seasonal luxury hotel in 1916. In the 1950s it became upscale housing for people over fifty-five and was in operation year-round. That eventually became unprofitable, and the building returned to being a seasonal hotel; but it catered to senior adults of more modest means. The building changed owners several times. It eventually went into foreclosure and was finally abandoned. The Sunset sat vacant for five years and during that time the structure began to take on a new life as an illegal residence for the homeless. It was also used by SWAT teams as a training site. Time had not proven to be kind to the old hotel.

My friends asked if I would like to see the building, and I quickly accepted their invitation. The hotel was going through major structural repairs when I first toured it—walls were missing, the floor was being shored up, and a huge hole in a wall marked where a fireplace had once stood. While there were hints of dignity here and there, it was hard to imagine this had ever been a luxury establishment.

The hope was to have the renovations finished in about a year, but it took much longer than expected. It was three years before the work was finally completed. The Crystal Bay Hotel opened on October 15, 2015.

After my visit to the hotel I was even more intrigued by it. I started doing some research and it didn't take long to learn that there were wonderful stories connected to the Sunset Hotel and the people behind it. As I followed the stories, they led me on a fascinating journey into the past.

The Guest Who Refused to Leave is historical fiction. The narrator, Clara, Thomas, Adeline, Homer, Marie and Joseph are characters created to tell the hotel's story. The other characters were real people. While I tried to stay as close to facts as possible, I found it is very difficult to distinguish between what is fact, what is legend, and what is just a good story.

Tourism grew quickly in St. Petersburg after the advent of the Model T. In 1905 there were six hundred and seventy-five rooms for tourists, but by 1925 that number had grown to over seven thousand. There were fewer than twenty hotels and rooming houses when the Sunset Hotel was built in 1916. Two years later there were sixty-three, and by 1927 there were one hundred and twenty-three hotels and boarding houses.

In the early 1900's, traveling by train was the only way for most people to get to Florida. Hotels didn't open until just before Christmas and closed by the first of April. Rooms were sparsely furnished. The apartments at the Sunset contained a folding bed, a telephone, hot and cold running water, and kitchen appliances. Tenants had to supply everything else. Guests, who were mostly older and well-to-do, arrived with large amounts of personal luggage and furnishings.

Local officials often overlooked the consumption of alcohol during Prohibition. Federal officials tried to enforce laws but liquor seems to have been plentiful in the area. Many establishments had a hiding place for alcoholic beverages. At the Sunset a secret room lined with shelves was found behind a closet in the lobby.

Tent City only lasted for one year in St. Petersburg. There was too much opposition to it from people who felt the Tin Can Tourists were freeloaders. The next year, however, many local residents set up private tourist camps on their property. Those were the forerunners for Florida's RV parks.

Tocobaga Indians lived at the site on Elbow Lane and they had burial grounds there. The area is said to be haunted. Walter P., with no regard for the people who had once lived there, leveled the land to build his complex. Restaurants, for some reason, do seem to have a hard time staying in business at the location, and employees like to tell of strange happenings in the building.

Elbow Lane is accepted as the landing site of Pánfilo de Narváez. The stories about Narváez, Juan Ortiz, Hirrihigua and his daughter are supposed to be true. However, where Hirrihigua lived on the Pinellas Peninsula is debatable. Several places claim to be the site; I chose to put him at Jungle Prado. The spelling of the names Hirrihigua and Mocoso also depend on which of the accounts you are reading.

Jungle Prado was the name Walter P. gave his complex. Years ago someone misspelled or changed the 'o' at the end of Prado to an 'a' and it became the accepted spelling. In the book, Jungle Prado refers only to the complex at Elbow Lane and Park Street.

Flamingos continue to fly across the ceiling in the entry hall at the Admiral Farragut Academy. The courtyard with the fountains, that so many people enjoyed years ago, is still there. Thanks to YouTube music from the Jungle Hotel and the Gangplank nightclub, played by Earl Gresh and his Gangplank Orchestra, can still be heard by listeners today.

Jack Taylor liked to be called 'Handsome Jack.' When he suddenly left St. Petersburg leaving behind massive debts, Walter P. claimed to have been shocked. He went to New York City, after it became obvious that no effort was being made to refinance the loans, and stayed with Jack for several months. As he sorted through records, Walter P. learned that his friend's name was an alias and his financial record was anything but sound.

While Walter P. was there, Jack decided to marry the international opera singer, Frieda Hemple. The marriage fell through on their wedding day when she realized he had no money. Jack seems to have disappeared after Walter P. returned home. He probably changed his name again and moved someplace where no one knew him.

Evelyn DuPont did remarry. Hopefully to someone more suited to her.

Al Capone came to the area occasionally, and he and Babe Ruth were supposed to have been friends. There are many stories about the houses and properties that Al Capone owned or lived in while he was in St. Petersburg, but what is fact and what is fiction has blurred over time.

The Gehrigs did not stay at the Sunset Hotel as far as anyone knows. However, they did have to find another place to stay after Lou got married, so it's fun to think it could have been at the Sunset. Christina calling Babe Ruth a 'giant' is fictional, but she did always called him 'Jidge.' She never forgave Eleanor for marrying her son.

There is no definite proof that Babe Ruth ever stayed at the Sunset Hotel, but longtime residents of the area are insistent that he did. There are accounts of where he stayed for every year but 1925, so he may have stayed at the Sunset that year. It would have given him and Helen the privacy they needed as they tried to work things out. It was also known that the Yankee management liked to house their star player away from the rest of the team so his questionable behavior didn't influence his teammates. The Sunset would have been a perfect choice. Babe may have later rented a suite at the hotel for his family. His daughter Julia has mentioned that they stayed at several different hotels when the family came down during spring training.

I owe thanks to so many people: my family and writing group for encouraging me and keeping me going, family and friends who read the manuscript and made suggestions and corrections, an editor whose help was invaluable, and the staff at the Crystal Bay who have patiently answered questions and looked up information for me. Special thanks go to Chef John Rivard for sharing recipes. The St. Petersburg History Museum, the University of South Florida archives, and Hillsborough Library were so helpful in aiding me with finding pictures and information.

But most of all, thanks go to Mark and Lee Tong for restoring a wonderful old hotel and not tearing it down.

Clara and her friends are very grateful.

68536563R00101

Made in the USA
Charleston, SC
16 March 2017